IN LOVE WITH THE RODEO RIDER

AN ALASKA SUNRISE ROMANCE

MELISSA STORM

Editor: Stevie Mikayne

Cover & Graphics Designer: TM Franklin

Proofreader: Falcon Storm

Partridge & Pear Press
PO Box 72
Brighton, MI 48116

To the boy who was my first kiss.
I think his name might have been Kevin?

And to the man who gets all my kisses from now until
eternity. Mr. Storm for the win!

ABOUT THIS BOOK

Louise Gordon left her small Alaska hometown during high school and vowed never to look back. Unfortunately, she has no choice when she is called in to settle the estate of a great aunt she hardly knew. With her best friend in tow, she reluctantly takes a trip across the country and back into her past—planning to return to her fast-paced Manhattan life as quickly as possible. Add in the rodeo star with whom she shared her first kiss so many years ago and a mechanical bull ride gone awry, and away we go.

This quick, light-hearted romance from a New York Times bestselling author is sure to put a smile on your face and a song in your heart!

*L*ouise's cell phone buzzed. She glanced at the out-of-area number and groaned, then sent the call straight to voicemail. But then it rang again, and again.

She hated when her assistant piped business calls to her personal line. Still, she could either answer or let it buzz for the rest of the day.

"Louise Gordon," she snapped, hoping her irritation showed.

"Louise? Sorry to bother you like this. But I'm calling about an urgent matter."

"Sorry, who is this?"

"This is Bill Ringstead of Ringstead and Associates, here in Anchorage."

Anchorage, her former hometown, the city she'd

vowed to forget when her family relocated to New York during her sophomore year of high school.

But now her past was calling. *Literally*.

This couldn't be good.

Mr. Ringstead continued, his voice friendly even though hers wasn't. "My firm represented your late aunt, Madeline Gordon. She's just passed on, but before that she instructed that no one was allowed to handle her estate but you. So how soon might you be able to make a trip out our way?"

Unbelievable.

She hadn't even spoken with her Great-Aunt Madeline for more than fifteen years, and had only met her a few times before that. Louise had never belonged in Alaska and had been all too happy to escape it when her father's company relocated them to Manhattan. No way she'd be going back.

"Can't you just handle the estate in my place? I'll sign off on whatever you need."

"I'm sorry, but your aunt's instructions were very clear. It can only be you. Think you can make it out next week?"

Louise wracked her brain for an excuse. This did not come at a good time. The hunt for her firm's next partner was well underway, and she'd been pulling out all the stops to make sure that partner would be her.

Randomly disappearing to handle an out-of-town family matter could only hurt her case.

But still family was family, and she'd hate to let her parents down by not at least making some effort to follow Aunt Maddie's wishes. She sighed, feeling her resolve crumble into dust.

"I'll need to move some things around, but fine. I'll see you in a week."

"We'll expect you then. You take care now. Bye."

Click.

What had she just agreed to? Her client roster was already filled to the brim, she was right in the thick of doing everything she could to land that new partner position, and besides, estate law wasn't even her focus.

A nagging feeling tugged at the back of her mind. Would she run into *him*? Her thoughts drifted back to his warm, chocolate eyes and confident smirk.

Stop being crazy. He must have moved on by now. Too much time had passed, and besides, he'd never been able to stay in one place for too long.

Well, good riddance. One less thing she'd have to deal with on her big return to Alaska.

～

*T*he sun beat down on Brady's shoulders. Beautiful day for a ride, he thought, slipping his cowboy hat onto his shaggy dark hair.

Fair-goers crowded into the stadium and watched the between-act clowns dance and tidy up. He knew the growing crowd was really here for him, though. He'd had some truly amazing rides, earning the high score almost every time he saddled up. Wherever he went, the crowds followed, especially around these parts where everyone wanted to root for the local boy.

Of course, they came to see him for other reasons, too. Years of riding had given him strong arms and an even stronger torso. It was too bad he had to stay covered up for safety reasons, because he loved showing off the body he'd earned through so much hard work and dedication.

Besides, the ladies just couldn't get enough of him —and he couldn't get enough of them.

A trio of gorgeous, leggy women—buckle bunnies, his absolute favorite rodeo perk—made their way over to where he stood outside the stables, checking over his harness and tie to make sure everything was set for his ride. This personal attention to detail was part of what made him so successful in work and elsewhere.

"Hi, Brady," they trilled in unison. Confidence. He

liked that in a woman. He liked it even better in three of them at once.

"Ladies." He tipped his hat in their direction. Man, they were gorgeous—especially the one with curly ringlets and large, cobalt eyes.

"What are you doing after the show?" she asked, pouting her lips seductively.

He was just about to answer that he'd be going out with them, of course, when a figure in the distance caught his eye. He shifted his gaze just to the right of his girls' heads and studied the gorgeous creature on the horizon.

Weezy.

Wow, it was really her. He hadn't seen her since she'd moved away in high school, but she'd stopped talking to him years before that. Of course, he'd never stopped trying to get back on her good side. As attractive as he found confidence, he needed a challenge every once in a while, too. And he'd never found another that rivaled Weezy.

He watched as she strode across the fairgrounds as if she owned the place—confident and hard-to-get— the perfect pursuit. Wasn't it just like her to turn up right as he was settling into his old, familiar rut? He grinned, remembering their last exchange, the one in which he'd shown up at her parents' place right before the cab that would take her away toward her new life. He begged her to give him another chance, to at least write him or call, but she just shook her head and got in the cab with her parents and drove out of his life— although not for good, apparently.

The girls turned to follow the path of his eyes as he studied Louise from a distance. "Who's that?" one of them asked with a sneer.

But Brady didn't have the time or heart to answer. He couldn't tear his eyes away from this gorgeous blast from his past.

Louise had grown up nicely. He loved her out-of-place pencil skirt and purple blouse. Showed how different she was from every random beauty queen that paraded across his path. Those legs, those hips, that short, striking haircut that perfectly contrasted her creamy skin. Clearly, she hadn't spent much time outdoors since they'd parted, and he intended to fix that straight away.

Only...

"You're up next, Rockwell," the show's lackey came up and slapped him on the back. "Let's get goin'."

"I'll be seeing you around," he told the girls as he headed to work—still unable to tear his eyes away from Weezy.

A few moments later, the announcer's voice

boomed over the stadium speakers. "And now it's the time you've all been waiting for! Announcing our favorite bad boy, Bucking Brady Rockwell."

He took a deep breath, as the gate released him into the ring.

~

*T*he cinnamony scent of fresh-fried elephant ears swirled around Louise's head as dust kicked up from the fairgrounds and whipped about in the wind.

"I can't believe we're at a real-life rodeo," her friend Missy gushed. She'd been born and raised in New York, and had insisted she come along for the journey the moment Louise had told her about the plan for a visit to Anchorage. "I didn't know Alaska was so country."

Louise's heel snagged on a discarded cotton candy cone. "Yeah, well... Thanks for coming along with me. This trip would have been unbearable without you."

"Hey, I needed a break, too. Wedding planning is so much harder than you'd think. Maybe I should just let my sisters plan it. They love this stuff, but all it does is make my head spin."

Louise felt every man's eyes turn toward them as

they entered the stadium and took their seats. While Louise commanded the attention of everyone who dared enter the courtroom, Missy tended to have the same effect twenty times over, no matter where they went. It was hard *not* to stare at the beautiful up-and-coming actress as she passed through, full of confidence in knowing exactly who she was. Sometimes, Louise found herself staring, too.

But she loved the way Missy shook her life up. Sure, they both clocked long hours at work, but her friend always found new ways to pull Louise away from the office and get her out on the town. In fact, that's what she had done the moment they arrived in Anchorage.

"We're here!" Missy trilled as the plane touched down on the runway. "What should we do first?"

Louise set her book down, making sure to hold her place with her thumb as she talked to Missy. "Let's go straight to check out the rental place, order takeout, and unpack our bags. Have a quiet night in. I'm so close to finishing this book and really want to know what happens. We'll be in town for a few days, and I promise we'll find something fun to do. It's just that, aren't you supposed to be taking a break from all the chaos of your life?"

Missy took out her phone, and moments later was

sticking it in Louise's face and waving it around. "Oh, the rodeo is in town! We are so going."

Louise laughed. "Okay, okay. We'll go."

They'd stopped quickly by the rental to drop off their bags, and then come straight to the fairgrounds. Missy was thrilled by their surroundings, but Louise couldn't help searching the many faces in the crowd.

Would he be here? No, he'd probably moved back to Austin long ago. Besides, he'd never been one to blend into the crowd. If he were here, he'd make absolute certain he had everyone's attention—including hers.

The announcer's voice boomed over the speakers, "It's the time you've all been waiting for!" Cheers rose from the crowd as they stomped their feet on the bleachers and chanted.

Louise missed the name of the performer in all the ruckus that ensued, but when he came tearing into the ring, she recognized him at once. *Brady.*

The bronco moved at a furious pace, but it was as if time slowed around them. Louise focused on Brady's hips as they rose up and down to accommodate the bucking movements, one hand gripped the saddle refusing to let go while the other held steady high over his head, his muscular legs hugging tight to the horse.

It was a sight to behold.

But this was crazy... She dated wealthy men in business suits who rode in luxury cars, not cowboys from her past life. But, still, there was no denying Brady's rugged, manly appeal as he worked the bucking horse to his will. She wouldn't put up nearly as much of a fight if she had the chance...

The chance to what?

She was *not* that girl anymore. She'd moved on to bigger and better things. She'd chased her dreams and caught them. So why couldn't she tear her eyes from this reckless boy from her past?

She wasn't ready to settle down. At least not until she'd settled comfortably into the partner role at her firm—that is if this whole interruption hadn't completely botched her chances altogether. But still there'd be other firms, and they'd be lucky to have her. And when she was ready, there would be other men, more compatible men.

This one was definitely off limits.

2

"One Mississippi ..." Brady muttered each count under his breath as he inhaled, exhaled, leaned forward and back, swayed left and right.

"Two Mississippi, three..." The bronco kicked and spun beneath him, but Brady anticipated his movements and clung tighter with every twist and turn. They didn't call him Bucking Brady Rockwell for nothing.

He trained hard before the show, and relied on that training when go-time rolled around. Then he would completely let himself go, let himself get absorbed into the horse, become a part of it. His mind stayed blank while his instincts took over. He just had to focus on the count.

"Four Mississippi..."

The audience blurred before him as the bronco took off in a series of tornado-like spins. A flash of purple caught his eye. He squinted for a better look on his next turn-through, and, sure enough, Weezy stood wearing that same purple silk blouse that would, no doubt, get destroyed by the dusty fairground winds.

"Five..."

Her eyes were wide as she watched him, a slight smile playing at her lips.

His heart picked up its pace and his palms grew sweaty. All these years later and she could still do a number on him.

Speaking of numbers, where was he in the count again? Six. No seven. Had it been eight yet?

That momentary lapse was all it took. He'd lost his sync with the bronco and got tossed.

Hard.

The audience moaned in disappointment. Not only wouldn't he be winning as expected, but he'd also managed to get himself disqualified—something he'd hardly done even in his rookie days.

The medics rushed over to check him for bumps, scrapes, broken bones. "Looked like a hard fall. You all right, Brady?"

He answered their questions distractedly as he

searched for that familiar swatch of purple in the audience, but Weezy had disappeared.

"We about done here, fellas?" he grumbled. Not only were they in his way, but the fact they seemed insistent on checking up on him was a huge embarrassment.

"You know we can't hurry through our checks. Just give us a moment here, and we'll be set."

As the medics continued making slow work of his examination, Brady practiced what he'd say once he caught up with her. Because there was no question, he *would* be catching up with her again.

His pulse quickened at the thought, and one of the medics made a note on his chart.

"What's got you so worked up today, hey?"

Brady let the question roll off him with a smile, but inside a million thoughts clawed to get out. Why was it that he could get any woman he wanted without a second thought, but could only focus on this one out-of-reach girl from his past? And why was he already as tongue-tied as he'd been back in his school days when he'd first asked if he could kiss her on the playground?

Well, tongue-tied or not, he refused to miss the chance to follow up with the girl who could take his breath away faster than a hoof to the chest. One way or another, he'd find something to say.

⌒

"*I* can't watch this anymore," Louise declared, getting up and pushing her way toward the end of the bleachers where she and Missy sat. As they made their way toward the exit, a collective gasp rose from the crowd. Louise looked over just in time to see Brady get thrown from his feisty bronco.

Her heart ached, just as she was sure every single part of his body did. This is what he does for a living, she reminded herself. He chose this. He knew the risks when he saddled up. In fact, his insistence on putting himself in harm's way was part of the reason they hadn't worked out.

She still remembered the time Brady had convinced each of their classmates to pay a dollar to watch him do a backflip off the top of the monkey bars.

Sure, he'd pulled it off, but he'd also broken his leg in the process.

Of course, he should have listened to her when she told him what a terrible idea it was, but then again that was Brady. If he wasn't doing something crazy, stupid, dangerous, then he wasn't living.

She paused long enough to make sure he was okay

now—long enough for her friend to realize something was up.

"A cowboy, huh?" Missy jabbed at Louise playfully. "He's totally gorgeous. I can see why you're smitten."

"Smitten, Missy? Really?" Louise rolled her eyes and strode briskly ahead. Why did she still care? She shouldn't give a lick about what happened to him after the way he'd treated her, but somehow, she couldn't help herself.

With her long legs, Missy easily matched her pace. "So, you don't deny it? I mean, why would you? That man is God's gift to women everywhere."

Louise shook her head. "If you say so."

"I can tell you like him, so dish already. Don't hold out on your best friend!" Missy offered Louise her signature pout, the one that landed her role after role and made her one of the top rising stars in the film industry.

"Look, Missy, I love you, but I'm not here to rehash the past, and I'm definitely not here to flirt with some rough-and-tumble cowboy, okay?"

"Okay, okay. I just want you to be happy the way I am." Missy sighed as she looked down at the magnificent diamond wrapped around her finger. "But I'll drop it, I swear. Ooh, look! Let's play some Skee Ball."

They paid the carny, and Louise stood back as

Missy wound up and tossed the worn, brown ball toward the loops at the end of the small runway.

Louise giggled as the ball rebounded and flew back. "It's not baseball."

Missy stuck out her tongue and threw again, this time scoring ten points.

"Give it another try, darlin'," the carny coaxed. "I bet you'll get fifty this time. Just focus on where you want the ball to go, then give it a good, firm toss."

Missy drew the ball toward her chest and took a deep, meditative breath. She was so competitive that even this silly game was approached just as seriously as one of her casting calls. Of course, Louise would have handled it the exact same way—except that she'd land a fifty pointer her first time out of the gate. Skee Ball had always been one of her favorite pastimes at the county fair.

"Go, Missy! You can do it!" Louise cheered and gave a small jump, enjoying the fact that her friend was every bit as much of a fish out of water here as she was.

Missy exhaled and released the ball. It zoomed down the track and landed in the large, outer loop once again.

"That's another ten points for you, darlin'. But I think you deserve a prize anyway." The carny smiled, revealing tobacco-stained teeth, and used a long hook to grapple a large plush toy for Missy.

"Oh, I love it so much!" Missy cooed and hugged the pink unicorn to her chest as soon as he offered it to her.

"Nice try, rookie," Louise joked, giving her friend a congratulatory pat on the back. "Now let me show you how it's really done."

"I can take it from here," said a low, husky voice from behind them.

Louise spun, recognizing the familiar boy's voice wrapped within its deeper, more adult version.

Brady's boots left a trail of starry imprints on the ground behind him. Dirt clung to his jeans and flannel shirt while sweat clung to his brow—yet somehow, he managed to look irresistibly handsome covered head to toe in grime.

"I don't believe I've had the pleasure," he said, taking Missy's hand. "They call me Bucking Brady Rockwell. Pleased to meet ya." His teeth shone brightly against his tanned features.

"Charmed, I'm sure," Missy said affecting a Southern drawl she probably hadn't used since her role in a stage remake of *Steel Magnolias*.

"Weezy." He turned to Louise and laid a kiss on the back of her hand. "It's been a long time."

The warm kiss lit her skin on fire. Surely, he hadn't had this same effect on her as a girl. She flushed, but then reminded herself that if she could handle the most belligerent opponents in court, then surely, she could handle a simple conversation with this harmless flame from her past.

"Actually, it's Louise now."

"Nah, I think you'll always be Weezy to me." He winked with a self-assurance she found irritating.

She frowned. "I'm not that little girl you once knew, Brady. A lot has changed since then."

"Well, you're still the most beautiful girl around. No offense, ma'am." He quickly smiled toward Missy. "So how much else could have changed?" He ran his eyes up and down her lean body and gave a grunt of approval.

Louise looked away, embarrassed by his attentions. "Well, for one thing I'm a woman, and I'd prefer you treat me like one rather than some hunk of meat."

His dark eyes peered out from beneath his cowboy hat, and a boyish smirk spread across his face. "I can treat you like a queen, Weezy. Just give me one night, and I'll—"

"How dare you talk to me that way! Just because I was interested in sixth grade doesn't mean I'm interested now." Louise crossed her arms over her chest and took a step back. She couldn't believe he'd talked to her that way, especially considering their history.

A frown overtook Brady's handsome features. "Wait, I didn't mean—"

"I'm with her on this. You can't talk to my friend that way," Missy cut in. "And how dare you call me, 'ma'am'? I'm only twenty-eight!"

"Please just hear me out," Brady drawled, but his attempt at charm was lost on them.

"Actually, I think we've heard enough. Ready to go home, Missy?"

She linked arms with her friend and strode away, but internally she felt relieved. *Thank you, Brady, for being such a chauvinistic perv. Now I'll have no trouble getting you off my mind, focusing on my work, and getting out of this crappy little town as fast as humanly possible. Good riddance.*

"Yuck. What a creeper." Missy brought a finger to her face and made a gagging sound.

"I honestly have no idea what I ever saw in him," Louise said as she hopped into their rental truck and revved up the engine. "Well, he's in the past for a reason. And looks like he's staying there for good." Louise peeked in the rearview mirror, but Brady was nowhere to be seen.

~

"*D*ang it." Brady cursed under his breath and kicked at a candy apple core that littered the ground. *What was I thinking? Of course I mucked it up the first chance I got.*

A classy woman like Louise needs to be treated with respect. She needs...

"Hey, I waited for you after the show. Are you all right?" The cobalt-eyed blonde swung her hips in a purposeful strut as she made her way over to him.

Great, this is just what I need. I need to move fast if I want to give my apologies to Weezy. Seriously, what in the heck was I thinking? It would've been better to say nothing at all! Now she's probably thinking about the last time, we... And why we... I messed up big time.

Brady plastered a smile across his face. Well, he could put on a show, too.

Or maybe this is what I need... Weezy—no, Louise, *she asked me to call her Louise*—clearly wasn't falling for his charm, or lack of it. Might as well move on to the next pretty young thing that trod his way, and—lookie here—she was standing before him that very moment.

"I think I'll be just fine." He fixed his eyes on the woman's mouth as he continued. "That is, if you'll keep me company this evening to make sure I'm all right." He held open his arms, and she took the invitation, snuggling into his side and looking up at him as if he were the only thing that mattered in the world.

See, why couldn't Louise be like that?

His new lady companion said something in a high-pitched trill, but he missed it.

"How's dinner sound?"

Again, he missed her words, but her sultry smile said it all.

He walked with her to the parking lot as she chattered on at a galloping pace, but, no matter how much he tried to focus, he just couldn't get Louise off his brain.

Looked like it was going to be a long night, after all.

3

*L*ouise squinted at the glowing red alarm clock. Only five in the morning, but she was wide awake, thanks to the four-hour time difference between New York and Alaska. They didn't need her in the office until nine, and she had no doubt Missy would sleep in as long as she could, so she crept out of the house and headed to the closest megastore for a quick supply run.

She'd already prepped ingredients for a salmon dinner, packed a lunch for the day ahead, and set about fixing a four-course breakfast by the time Missy appeared at the top of the stairs.

"Do I smell bacon?" she asked, rubbing the sleep from her eyes. Even though Louise had a full face of makeup and Missy had none, there was no question as to which of them looked more glamorous that early morning.

"And moose sausage and eggs benedict and pancakes," Louise answered as she deftly flipped a cake in the griddle.

"Moose sausage, huh? You can take the girl out of Alaska, but you can't take the Alaska out of the girl."

Louise chortled. "More like you can take the girl away from her law firm, but you can't take her law firm away from the girl. I wish you had let me bring my case notes. I did at least finish my book, but after that I was up for hours with nothing better to do than cook."

"Seems like it worked out well for me then." Missy grabbed a piece of bacon and dabbed off some of the grease before crunching into it. "Besides, you're here to work anyway, and you needed *some* form of break. All those eighty-hour workweeks just aren't good for you."

"You're one to talk about work-life balance." Louise smirked as she laid the finished griddle cake on an empty plate.

"Hey, you know things have been different since Jordan stole my heart away. Besides I didn't bring an ounce of work with me in my carry-on. You know that means I win, right?"

"Oh, so there aren't any scripts hidden in your suitcase or on your phone?"

Missy shook her head emphatically, and Louise sighed.

"Fine, you win. Now have another slice of bacon. You could use it."

"You don't have to tell me twice. You know I'm a sucker for bacon." Missy fixed them both full plates while Louise poured orange juice into two green plastic tumblers.

"I don't have anywhere to be, so make mine a mimosa."

"Oh, that reminds me, I picked up a bunch of movies while I was at the store. You know, all the stuff you can't usually find on Netflix." She motioned toward a brown paper bag, and Missy popped up to grab it.

"*Sweet Home Alabama, The Notebook, Never Been Kissed, 27 Dresses...* Jeez, Louise! Looks like you had romance on the brain."

Louise chuckled and popped a forkful of eggs into her mouth. "Hey, I know how to keep my woman happy."

"Spoiling me with home-cooked meals and romantic comedies. Jordan better watch out!" Missy took a long swig of her mimosa and put her feet up on the adjacent chair. "A girl could get used to this."

"I wanted to make sure that at least you had a good

time while I'm stuck in the office all day." She frowned and shot her friend an apologetic look.

"Don't act like you don't love it, Ms. Workaholic."

"Speaking of which, I have to scoot. See you tonight, okay?" She gave Missy's shoulder a squeeze as she passed by.

"Yup, I'm all set here." Missy grabbed a leftover forkful of eggs from Louise's plate. "See ya in a few."

Louise gave Missy a quick kiss on the top of her head before charging through the door. Even though her temporary office was less than a five-minute drive from their rental home, she felt rushed. She needed to allow at least forty-five minutes each day to get to her Manhattan firm bright and early before the partners arrived.

The large truck felt far too bulky for her liking. Then again, being huddled in a subway car with dozens of other agitated New Yorkers didn't exactly make for a comfortable commute either. A call came through the system's Bluetooth, and she recognized the number at once.

Her boss. *Crap.*

"Louise Gordon," she answered, attempting to sound happy about the call.

"Louise, listen, we're having some trouble with the Kleinmann case. Can you give me a quick rundown?"

She ran through the most pertinent facts quickly. Of course, the Kleinmann account was zooming forward quickly without her.

Of course.

This was her biggest client, and not being there when he needed her would look unprofessional to the partners.

She rolled past a bright, little coffee shack. The aroma of dark roast and donuts wafted in through the window, which she'd cracked to help clear her head. Further down the road, she spied the local townsfolk bustling about as they prepared for the day ahead. A familiar form emerged from among them. His muscular legs hardly touched the pavement as he flew down the street at a sprint.

Louise slowed to get a better look. Just because she'd sworn off talking to him didn't mean she couldn't appreciate looking at him from a distance.

"Gordon, did you get that?" Her boss sounded agitated.

"I'm sorry, get what?"

"I need you to email me the documents for Kleinmann right away. By ten please. We need to move forward on this, and we need to move forward now. I know you're on vacation, but—"

"I'm not on vacation."

Her boss sighed, and she could tell he'd already lost his patience with her. "Yeah, but you're not here, either."

"I'm sorry about that. Of course, give me five minutes, and you'll have them."

"Good." The phone clicked, and the local radio station took back over the speakers.

Brady waved in her direction.

She didn't know what to do, so she threw him an awkward smile and waved back, then watched as he continued down the street in the opposite direction, his jogging shorts tugging at his gorgeous backside.

HONK!

"Sorry, sorry," Louise called to the driver she'd just cut off at the four-way stop. When she glanced back in her rearview mirror, she saw that Brady was laughing at her. This was not a good start to her day—not a good start at all.

4

—————

$\mathcal{B}$y the time Louise trudged home from her temporary office, night had already enveloped the sky and a full blanket of stars twinkled brightly above.

Missy, still in her pajamas, swiped at tears as *The Notebook* reached its dramatic conclusion. When the end credits filled the screen a few moments later, she turned to Louise and asked, "Do you think Jordan loves me like that? Like how Noah loved Allie?"

"Obviously." Louise choked back a laugh while her friend let her tears flow freely.

"Yeah." She sniffed. "Me, too." And just like that, her tears dried up and she popped to her feet, dragging Louise toward the stairs. "Now, c'mon. I need a night out, and so do you."

"Don't you at least want to hear about my day?" Louise asked as Missy rifled through her suitcase.

"Nope, work stays at the office. Now it's time to have some fun. *Here*." She thrust a sequined, backless number toward Louise. "Put this on, freshen up your makeup, and meet me in five. We're going to the bar."

Louise tugged at the hem of the shirt she'd borrowed from Missy as they entered the bar later that evening. Way too flashy, but she knew better than to argue when it was easier to just play along. Missy had never steered her wrong before—at least not when it came to letting loose and enjoying herself.

When they walked into Jake's Watering Hole, the local honky-tonk bar, all eyes turned toward them—or, more aptly, toward Missy. Louise smiled shyly and followed Missy over to the bartender.

"Two screaming orgasms," Missy announced, slamming a twenty down onto the leather-trimmed counter.

Louise rolled her eyes and hoped no one had overheard.

Just then, a man wearing a business suit brushed Missy's twenty aside and slapped down two hundred-dollar bills. "Why stop at two? I can treat you to as many of those there orgasms as you'd like."

"Sure." Missy flashed her famous smile toward the

generous stranger. "As long as it's just booze you're talking about. I'm an engaged woman."

"Engagements can be broken." The man wrapped his arms around Missy's waist and leaned in toward her neck, taking a deep, lusty breath.

"Not this one. But, hey, thanks for the drinks." She pulled Louise by her purse strap to a booth in the far corner of the open space, sashaying as they retreated.

The bartender brought over their drinks and an order of loaded potato skins. "On the house," she said, pointing her chin in the direction of the appetizer. "My way of apologizing for that creep earlier. This is a friendly establishment—but not *that* friendly. Anyway..." She plopped a pair of small plates before them. "Your drinks are paid for, for the night and then some, so enjoy. Just holler when you're ready for a refresher. I'll be around."

Missy speared a potato skin and drove it into her mouth. "My favorite," she said around the bite.

Something still bothered Louise. Missy told Brady off for showing even the slightest hint of disrespect, but had endured much worse from the man at the bar without so much as speaking up for herself. What made it different for her? Louise couldn't resist asking. "How do you just let it roll off you like that?"

"What, the creeper? Occupational hazard, unfortunately. I can let it upset me, or I can just move on with my life. Bottoms up, Weezy." She giggled and motioned for the bartender to bring another round.

"Only if you promise never to call me that again," Louise hissed. She plugged her nose and let the hot liquor slide down her throat. She was much more of a Chianti kind of girl, but when in Rome—or in Anchorage as the case may be.

"Make them Jacks," she hollered over the rising noise of the bar once the sting of the liquor had worn off.

"Now that's more like it." Missy pulled out her ponytail and gave her head a good, solid shake, causing her gorgeous blonde hair to cascade down her back.

"So that cowboy. *Dish*." Her eyes glowed in the dimly lit bar.

"There's not much to tell." Louise tucked a stray tendril of hair behind her ear and forked idly at the spuds.

"Well then, it won't take very long to tell me everything."

"You sure do know how to get your way."

"It's a talent." Missy winked and then motioned for Louise to get on with it.

"Well, I had a crush on him back in grade school, and when he asked me out, I said yes."

"Uh-huh."

"By then, we were in middle school. No one is actually all that serious then. We ended up dating for a year or so before drifting apart."

"What happened?"

"We just weren't right for each other. He was the jock, and I was the book nerd. None of our interests matched up."

"How very practical of you."

"Well..." Louise smiled and rolled her eyes. Missy was always calling her out on her lawyerly ways.

"Somehow I have a feeling you aren't telling me everything. What broke you up?"

"Really, that's everything." Louise didn't feel like rehashing the past, and she definitely didn't feel like reliving the moment that had broken them up for good. Still, she needed to throw Missy a bone here.

"Did I tell you he was my first kiss? Maybe that's why he's left such a lasting impression."

Missy's eyes glowed from across the table. "Your first! How was it?"

"Wet and kind of gross. We were only twelve. Neither of us knew what the hell we were doing back then."

"I bet he knows now."

Louise scoffed. "Yeah, a fact he is most definitely aware of."

"You've always liked the cocky ones before. Why not this time?"

"Seriously, Missy? You heard how he talked to me, and besides we come from two different planets."

"See, that's funny, because I thought you were both raised here in Anchorage." She fixed her friend with a knowing stare.

"You know what I mean. Anyway, I think I need another shot... Two more over here," she shouted.

"You think you can get off that easy? Well, think again."

Louise huffed. "What? That's everything, really."

"Everything except for why you're all flustered every time I mention his name."

"I am not!"

"*Brady*."

A lump formed in Louise's throat, but she swallowed it back down.

"Bucking Brady Rockwell." Missy chomped her teeth flirtatiously, and Louise couldn't keep a nervous heat from rising to her face. "See, see! Right there! Total flusterment."

"First, that's not a word. And, second, fine, he's a good-looking man. What more do you want?"

"For starters, you can admit that you totally want to jump his bones."

Louise shook her head in denial. Surely, her friend knew her better than this. "I'm not like that, and you know it."

"Yeah, but you like him. Admit it. *Admit it now*."

"And then you'll drop it?"

"Then I'll drop it."

Louise slammed another shot and when the sting had subsided said, "Okay, I like him."

Missy laughed. "Yeah. How much?"

She grabbed the next shot before the bartender could even place it on the table, and downed it fast. Her head began to spin, but she tried to ignore it. There was a reason she very rarely let any alcohol past her lips. She hated to lose control, hated to feel like her brain was trapped within a thick layer of fog.

Missy quirked an eyebrow and repeated her earlier request. "Tell me," she whined.

"I like him so bad I haven't been able to get him out of my head for hours. So much it took all my restraint to focus on the estate while I was at work today. So much that if he were here now, I'd..."

"You'd?"

"That I might even consider saying hi the next time I see him."

"Wow, how many shots have we had tonight? You're such an animal, Louise!"

"Shut up," Louise leaned over the table to shove Missy, and her shirt picked up some sour cream along the way.

"Awww, darn it!" She dabbed at it with some water, but the sour cream stayed, and the thin fabric soaked through to reveal her dark bra underneath.

"Hey, since you're already feeling a little crazy, and now you have a wet T-shirt to boot, why not take this wild night up a notch?"

Louise hobbled to her feet and put her hands on her hips. "Meaning?" she asked.

"*Ride the bull.* Giddy-up, let's go!" Missy hooted and pumped a fist in the air as she pushed Louise toward the center stage where the bulky, mechanical beast stood idle.

"Wanna make this interesting?" Louise asked, hitching up her jeans and striking what she hoped was a fierce pose. Missy had taught her so well.

"I already find this absolutely fascinating, but what else have you got?" Missy mirrored Louise's motions and laughed.

"Fifty to whoever stays on the longest. Me first."

"You've got it."

"And you're going down, Hollywood."

"Ha, we'll see about that!" Missy let out a full-bellied laugh as the wrangler let Louise into the padded ring and showed her how to mount the bull.

Louise clung tightly to her mount as it buzzed to life—at first slowly and then faster and faster until the entire room blurred around her. She could vaguely hear Missy's cheers in the distance, but tried not to focus on that. Louise never backed down once her competitive side came out to play. Besides her competitiveness was the very thing that made her successful in the first place—and it was the very thing that would ensure she won this particular challenge as well.

She swung her hips in tandem with the bull and circled her fist in the air as if slinging an invisible lasso. She was Wonder-freaking-Woman. Strong, sexy, invincible.

Is this how Brady felt every time he saddled up? Because if so, then she was definitely starting to understand. There was something about facing danger—no matter how small—that felt incredibly empowering.

She closed her eyes and basked in the moment, clinging to the bull for what felt like forever—until one wild twist proved to be too much, and she toppled off and landed on the mat below.

"Ouch," she moaned as the other bar-goers cheered and the wrangler announced that she'd managed to hang tight for sixteen-and-a-half seconds.

"You were awesome," Missy gushed, rushing into her line of vision. "Hey, are you okay?"

"I'm fine... I think," Louise took a deep breath and attempted to rise, but the room still spun around her, making that difficult.

"Allow me," a man said, offering his hand.

She grabbed on without a second thought, and a moment later she was standing full and tall and face-to-face with none other than Bucking Brady Rockwell.

Just one drink to clear my head. That's all I need.

Brady made his way to Jake's for the third time that week. When he wasn't on the road, the Watering Hole functioned as his second home. And he was beginning to feel like he might be in a rut.

Sure, his life was filled to the brim with adventure for those few seconds each week he was riding, but the rest of the time.... Yeah, definitely a rut.

Shelby served him up a tall, foaming glass of Kicker Session IPA from the tap and slid it over to his usual place at the bar. He hadn't even reached his stool yet when a commotion erupted from across the room.

He looked over just in time to see Weezy—his Weezy—mount the mechanical hulk of a bull. Funny how he thought of her as *his* Weezy when he was the one who'd gotten stuck on her. He only had a moment to appreciate the amusing sight of his high-strung sweetheart letting loose on that bull before she'd managed to slip off and cut her ride short.

He rushed to her side even though he saw her laugh and shake off the fall. Still, he needed any excuse he could get to talk with her. He needed a date, or at least closure. And he wouldn't be leaving without one or the other that night.

As he drew closer, he took a moment to appreciate her incredibly revealing outfit. The dark sequined number was definitely not something he'd have pictured her in before, but now that she was wearing it, he couldn't picture her in anything else.

She truly was a vision.

Louise struggled to gain a footing, but couldn't seem to lift herself from the floor. He offered his hand like any gentleman would.

"B-Brady?" She blinked, crimson blazed on her delicate cheeks.

"None other." He could have sworn that her shirt was soaked through, but he didn't want to make the same mistake he had during their last chance meeting by focusing on her body instead of her face—that face was the most beautiful part of her, after all. He saddled her with his most devilishly handsome grin, the one all the ladies swooned for.

But Louise didn't swoon. She scoffed. "I don't think so. Not after the way you talked to us the other day."

"I'm truly sorry, I am. In fact, that's part of why I came over here, to apologize. Can ya just give me another chance? Let me prove I'm not such a bad guy."

Louise puzzled over his words for a moment, and then a fire bloomed behind her normally soft eyes. "Buy us another round, and I'll think about it."

"I'm sorry to say, but it looks like you've already had quite enough."

Missy chuckled into the back of her hand. "She's about three drinks past *enough*."

"Well, then." Louise marched up to Brady and pushed her index finger into his chest. "If you won't comply with my demands, then I won't comply with yours."

"How very lawyer of you, Weezy," Missy interjected. "But, uh, we kind of need him."

"I don't need anybody. I can do it all myself."

"What are you even talking about? *Look*." Missy turned to Brady. "This is all my fault. I clearly let her drink way too much, and, well, now we need your help to get home."

"No, we don't. We're fine." Louise slurred her words as she argued.

"We are *so* not fine. I told you before we left that I can't drive a stick, and you're way too far gone."

"We could walk," Louise insisted. "It's only a few miles."

"At night, in the pitch black, in these heels? I think not." A mischievous grin crept across Missy's face. "Hey, remember, what you said you'd do if Brady showed up here tonight?"

Louise gasped and shook her head. "Fine, fine. You win, but, just so you know, it's because you fought dirty."

Brady had no idea what they were talking about, but he loved the pinkness that rose to Louise's cheeks as her friend teased her. And he loved that Missy seemed to be helping to push them together. That would make things so much easier. He smiled and looked from one woman to the other. "Does this mean I can drive you two home?"

"Sure, but we're taking my truck." Louise thrust the keys into his chest and sauntered toward the door. "Now, c'mon. We haven't got all night."

On the contrary, Brady thought. The night is just getting started.

❦

*B*rady drove the two women back to their rental home and walked them to the front stoop. He didn't want to leave them just yet, but he also knew Louise hadn't liked it when he'd been too forward the other day. He'd have to play it cool and gentlemanly if he were to stand even a prayer of a chance.

"Here we are! Home sweet home!" Louise pushed past him and fell into the front door while jamming her key in the knob. "So long, Brady. Thanks for the ride."

Missy gasped. "That's not very nice. He drove us all this way and didn't even get to finish his beer. The least we can do is invite him in for a nightcap."

Louise's eyes threw daggers her friend's way, but she just shrugged and said, "Fine. Come on in."

"Umm, is Sprite good?" Missy asked holding up the bottle of soda and reaching into the high cupboard for a glass.

"It's my favorite. How'd you know?"

"Apparently, it's Weezy's favorite, too. She's the one who made sure to pick some up."

"Don't call me that," Louise scolded.

Missy laughed and handed Brady his glass. "So... Louise tells me you two used to date?"

She'd set him up perfectly. Now he just had to deliver.

"Yup, she was my first love, this one. It's good to see you again by the way. I'm sorry about before."

Louise's entire face turned red and she sank back into her armchair as far as it would take her.

When it was clear she wouldn't be contributing to their conversation, he added, "You sure turned out nice. A lawyer, right? I always knew you were smart, and you're more beautiful than ever, too, by the way." He meant every word. He just wished he had a more poetic way to state his feelings. He had an inkling that type of thing would impress her.

Louise's face scrunched up as if too many emotions were fighting to make their way out. Part of him was thankful she'd had so much to drink, because it meant she was willing to give him this second chance, but another part of him desperately wished she was sober. He refused to take advantage of a drunk girl, no matter how much he wanted her—no matter how much he knew she wanted him, too.

Louise brought a hand to rest on her collarbone. "Th-thank you. You're not too hard on the eyes yourself."

Did she remember that was the same exact thing she'd said to him when he'd first told her how beautiful he found her? Did she remember when they first kissed on the playground after school, or when she'd let him hold her hand at the school assemblies?

The flush extended from her face down both of her arms. She clearly remembered, and now she was turning beet red before him.

"You look a little flustered, Louise. Maybe you'd feel better if we all took a nice soak in the hot tub?" Missy suggested.

"A hot tub, huh? Well, I'm definitely going to want to check that out," Brady said, watching as Louise got up and stormed away.

"Don't mind her," Missy apologized. "She really does like you. She just has a hard time letting herself relax sometimes. She's a good person. Actually, she's the best."

"I don't doubt that." Brady took a long drink from his soda and chuckled.

A few moments later, Louise reappeared, wearing a black halter-top bikini. His engine revved as he took in the sight of her fair skin contrasted with the dark fabric that left just enough to the imagination to help him maintain his composure.

She'd let her hair down, too. The short bob cut

curled around her chin, reminding him of the shy girl he'd once loved, the woman he could see himself beginning to love again. How was it that every single time he saw her she looked more beautiful than the last?

She tossed a pair of towels their way. "Surf's up, kids." Then walked out onto the deck, trailing a Betty Boop beach towel in her wake.

"Go," Missy urged. "I'll go grab my suit, and be right down."

Well, she didn't need to tell him twice. Brady slid open the glass door to the patio and found Louise already in the gurgling tub, an arm thrown up on either side of her as she continued to pull at her beer.

"You going to keep me waiting, or what?" Shedding her clothes also seemed to have shed her inhibitions. She kept her eyes fixed on him as he stripped down to his boxers and waded in to meet her.

"So, riding keeps you in shape, does it?" Her gaze flitted down to his chest before quickly averting in embarrassment. "They don't make them like you in New York," she mumbled.

He chuckled. "They don't make them like you anywhere in the whole wide world," he said as Louise drifted closer.

"So, you still think I'm pretty?"

He nodded. "Prettier than ever."

"And smart?"

"As a whip."

"And beautiful?"

"Unbelievably b—" He couldn't finish his short sentence, because the moment the question left her lips, she grabbed his face and pulled it toward hers for a kiss.

It took all his strength to push her gently away.

Hurt reflected in Louise's eyes as she studied him. "I don't understand. Don't you like me?"

"I like you so, so much. That's why I can't do this. Not while you're drunk."

"I'm not too drunk to know what I want," she protested.

"No, not like this. It's been fifteen long years since I saw you last, and I still can't get you off my brain. If we're going to do this, we've got to do it right. C'mon, I'm putting you to bed." He helped her out of the tub and wrapped the oversized towel around her.

She didn't put up too much of a fight as he coaxed her upstairs and led her to bed.

"Where are your pajamas?" he asked, rifling through her suitcase and dresser, but coming up short.

"I haven't got any." She bit her lip and crossed her

legs, glancing up at him from beneath long, dark lashes.

"Oh, no. You're not getting off that easy. *Here.*" He threw his own T-shirt her way. "Put this on."

She giggled as the cotton fabric pooled around her. Somehow seeing her in his simple white T-shirt was even more attractive than her little black bikini. He pulled on his jeans and flannel over-shirt, then tucked Louise under the covers and gave her a quick peck on the forehead.

"Good night, darlin'," he drawled, turning off the light behind him and making his way back through the house to the front door.

The warm summer air greeted him as he slipped out into the night, but he was still keyed up from the unbelievable encounter with Louise. Luckily, he had a several-mile walk back to the bar to help him cool down.

And, oh, how he needed it.

6

*T*he smell of freshly brewed coffee rose up through the ventilation system. A moment later, footsteps sounded on the stairs with a series of soft thuds.

"Knock, knock," Missy called as she padded into Louise's room to set a bottle of Aquafina and a cup of black coffee on the nightstand.

"Rise and shine!" she trilled, tugging at the blinds and letting the horrid sun into the room.

"Here, looks like you'll need this." She tossed a small bottle of pills Louise's way, and they hit her in the chest.

"*Ugh.* It's too early for this."

"Early? What time do you have to be in the office?"

Missy plopped down at the end of Louise's mattress and pulled her feet up underneath her.

Louise twisted the lid off the water and downed a couple of Tylenol before even venturing a glance at her clock.

Crap, it was already eight o'clock. She had an hour to pull herself together, shake off her hangover, and arrive bright-eyed and bushy-tailed at her temporary office for another fun-filled day of estate work.

"How late were we up last night, and why don't you look nearly as tired as I feel?"

"Me? I went to bed around midnight. I have no idea what time you went to bed, though. Hey, is Brady still around? I didn't see him when I got up."

Slowly, the events of the previous night started clicking together in Louise's mind. The drinks, the mechanical bull, the hot tub, going up to her room together.... "Oh, no... We didn't?"

Missy shook her head. "Don't look at me. I have no idea what happened once the two of you got in the hot tub. But knowing you, I doubt you have anything to worry about." She snickered for a moment before getting up and heading over to Louise's luggage.

"I'll find you something to wear. Why don't you hop in the shower and wash off that hangover scuzz?"

Louise yawned and stretched, but didn't want to think about the workday ahead—at least not until she'd made sense of the night behind her. "Missy, seriously, what happened last night?"

"I told you, I don't know. I saw you two flirting in the hot tub. Where you went from there, I have no idea."

"Why didn't you stop me? You knew how drunk I was!"

"Yeah, and I also knew how much you liked him and how much you just needed to let go and have some fun. What's the big deal? It's not like you have to see him again... Unless you want to?"

She ventured a smile. She knew exactly what she was doing, and unfortunately for Louise, once Missy set her mind on something, there was no turning back.

Still, it didn't mean she had to sit back and allow Missy to play chess with her love life. She was a queen, and she could make her own moves, thank you very much.

It was time to take charge of this situation with Brady once and for all—and she knew just what she needed to do.

"Of course, I want to see him again. In fact, I want to see him right now. He's got some major explaining to do." Louise took another swig of water and climbed out of bed. Much to her chagrin, she found that, rather than her favorite tank top and pajama bottoms, she was wearing an oversized white T-shirt that smelled like barbecue smoke and sweat. *Brady*.

Then it was officially decided. She was never *ever* drinking again.

"Is that his...?" Missy's voice trailed off, leaving the question to linger between them.

Louise hoped the annoyance that spread across her face was enough of an answer for Missy, because she needed to get out of there and find some answers for herself. She only hoped she'd be able to handle whatever truth she found out.

~

*B*rady hadn't gotten much sleep the night before, but that didn't stop his body from waking up with the sun like a well-oiled machine, or a strutting rooster, or something like that. He smiled as the events from the night before replayed in his mind.

A true saint, that's what he was. Louise had thrown herself at him, but, like a gentleman, he'd declined. Still, he had a feeling it would all be worth it when he saw Louise again.

He let his mind linger on her killer curves and

gorgeous smile before climbing out of bed and jamming his feet into his favorite pair of running shoes.

He had a feeling today would go down in history as one of his most epic days yet, but he couldn't let it get started without his morning run. A quick jog around the neighborhood would help clear his mind, energize him, get him ready for whatever sweetness lay ahead.

The morning sun shone bright as he made his way out the door. Brady turned to the left and headed toward the loop of the cul-de-sac. He'd been doing this same run for more than a decade, yet somehow it never got old.

As he passed his mother's home, he noted that she needed a fresh coat of paint on her shutters and vowed to return later that week to help her get the job done. Things hadn't been the same since his father passed a few years back, but luckily, he had been able to buy a home nearby and keep watch over his mom without invading her space too much.

While he was there for a visit, maybe he could plant some flowers in her window boxes as a surprise. She'd always loved tending to her peonies, but he hadn't seen any new blooms this past year. Yes, it was the little things that made the biggest difference when it came to his mother, or any woman for that matter.

He just had to figure out the best way to see Louise again. She was in town closing up some estate—maybe if he stopped by her office with a fistful of wildflowers....

Another turn to the left, and he was approaching the main road. The scents of fresh-baked bread and cinnamon rolls permeated his senses as he trod through the tiny downtown. He'd have to stop by later and see how business was doing for Chuck and his bakery this year. Of course, he could snag a treat or two while he was at it. He'd turned down enough treats the previous night to last him a lifetime.

As he neared his next turn, a yellow Silverado rolled into view. He recognized the truck instantly. After all, he'd been the one to drive it last night when neither Louise nor her friend could.

Sure enough, the vehicle slowed to a crawl and drove beside him as he continued his run. The window rolled down, and Louise called out to get his attention, unaware that she already had it.

He certainly hadn't expected to see her so soon after last night's encounter, but he wasn't going to look a gift horse in the mouth. He knew horses well enough to understand you had to look them straight in the eye and be forthright if you wanted any hope at all of taming them.

Women, too, actually.

"Good morning, darlin'," he called, keeping up his pace but turning briefly to smile at her.

Louise did not smile back. In fact, she scowled. He was just about to ask what had gotten her down, when she supplied a very loud and angry answer for him.

"Just what did you think you were doing last night?"

She paused and let out a huff.

He sputtered for an explanation. "I—"

"I'm not finished yet! You think that it's okay to take advantage of someone when they're drunk? I was clearly out of my mind and you know I'm not that kind of girl, but that didn't stop you from making your move, did it?"

"You seem to be under some kind of false impression here. We—"

"I know exactly what we did. Here, take your shirt back." She tossed the white cotton bundle at him, and it fell to the sidewalk.

Well, if this is how she was going to play it, he would definitely need to cut his run short to address a few key misunderstandings. He scooped up his shirt and put a hand on the passenger door of Louise's truck.

"I'm coming in." He reached through the open window and pulled up the lock.

"Like heck you are."

But he had already slid onto the bench seat and closed the door behind him.

Louise kept her eyes on the road as she accelerated through the light the moment it turned green. "I thought I made my feelings clear, but I guess they need to be repeated."

Brady chuckled.

"This is *funny* to you?"

"Well, for all the strife you're giving me, I almost wish I hadn't been such a gentleman."

"What?" Her tone softened, and she shot a furtive glance his way.

"Nothing happened. Not even a kiss. Although, believe me, you tried. Weezy, you were drunk as a skunk, and I like you too much to take advantage like that."

"Well, good. Thank you." Now her eyes softened, too. "Look, I'm sorry. Can we start over here?"

"Let's start over altogether. Let me take you out tonight on a proper date, one you'll remember on your own." He knew just where he wanted to take her, too, provided she said yes.

Louise was silent for a few beats. Probably thinking of the most diplomatic way to turn him down. But then she smiled and said, "Yeah. I'd like that."

7

*T*hat night's date with Brady helped Louise to pull through another long day of mucking about in her late aunt's incredibly tangled estate.

Aunt Madeline had such a long list of assets, it was ridiculous—and more than half of these assets were ones Louise never even knew she'd owned. Like the small farm out in Iowa, or the stake in a tech start-up in Silicon Valley.

Add to that her even longer list of debts and conditions, and they still hadn't even begun to tackle the will. *Soon.* They'd get there soon enough. For now, Louise could just enjoy her trip down memory lane with a certain debonair cowboy.

And by the time five o'clock rolled around, she was all too eager for a change of scenery.

"See you tomorrow, Bill," she sang as she stuffed her files back into her briefcase and strode toward the door.

At home, she found Missy sitting cross-legged on their large, leather ottoman with her computer perched on her lap. A bridal website was pulled up on the browser.

She startled as Louise closed the door behind her with a heavy thud. "Oh, it's just you. Is it evening already?"

"Yup."

Missy groaned. "I've spent all day looking for the perfect wedding dress, wedding theme, wedding favors, wedding whatever, and I still haven't settled on a single thing."

Louise dropped her briefcase to the floor and sat across from her friend on the couch. "Why not hire a wedding planner? You can certainly afford it."

"I've thought about it, but that's so impersonal, you know?" She pressed the laptop shut and pushed it aside. "Anyway, talk to me. I could use a change of pace."

Louise's voice trembled. "Actually...."

Missy rolled her eyes, but smiled. "You're ditching me for a date with Brady, right?"

"What—how did you know? I'm sorry, Missy, I feel awful, but—"

"But you really, really like him. And I'm really, really happy for you!" Missy looped her arms around Louise and gave her an affectionate squeeze.

Louise frowned. She deserved Missy's irritation, not her understanding. She'd been a horrible friend this week, probably longer if she really stopped to think about it. Still, she couldn't deny the pull of her heart toward Brady. She needed to see this through, if for nothing more than to get it out of her system, to finish what they'd started so many years ago. She glanced up at her friend.

"Are you sure? It seems like you've had a pretty rough day. I can cancel. I'll just need to—"

"What? Are you crazy? Don't do that! I'll probably call Jordan and talk to him for a few hours before turning in for the night. I miss him like crazy. Plus, I'm beat anyway." A wistful expression crossed her face as she said her fiancé's name. Louise doubted the two had ever been apart for a single day, much less several days on end, and it was all her fault that they were apart now.

"You're one hundred percent sure? I feel like an awful friend."

"Seriously, just shut up and go make yourself look fabulous." Missy bumped her shoulder and made a funny face.

Louise let out a deep breath. "Thank you! You're the best!"

"I know." Missy picked up her laptop again, then paused. "Hey, Louise."

"Yeah?"

"Just don't drink too much this time, okay?"

Louise tossed a throw pillow at Missy, and they collapsed in a fit of giggles.

A few minutes later, the doorbell chimed to the tune of Greensleeves.

"Crap, he's early! Buy me a few minutes, okay?" Louise rushed up the stairs and left Missy to deal with their guest.

She dabbed a fresh spray of perfume onto her wrists and ran her fingers through her short hair to get it to flip out at the ends the way she liked best. Her outfit from earlier that day, an A-line skirt and robin's egg blue blouse were just playful enough to work if she ditched the stuffy, khaki blazer. All she needed now was a cute pair of sandals to transform this office get-up into a date night ensemble. She dusted a bit of powder on her T-zone and applied fresh coats of lip gloss and mascara before heading downstairs.

Brady sat with Missy at the kitchen counter poring over something on her computer screen.

"That could work," he said as a white princess cut dress with a long train popped onto the display. He looked incredible in his faded jeans and dark plaid shirt.

She took a moment to appreciate him from afar before making her way over and placing a hand on his shoulder.

"Hmm, it's a little busy. Maybe this one?" Missy clicked and brought up a strapless number trimmed with pink pearls.

"Ready?" Louise offered him a placating smile as she came to stand next to them both. She still felt bad about the way she'd accused him of taking advantage of her earlier this morning. At least she hadn't made him wait long while she got changed.

As much of a perfectionist as she could be, she'd never been high maintenance when it came to her appearance. As long as her clothes and accessories looked nice and she'd had time to freshen up, Louise was good to go.

Brady stood and wrapped her in his arms, greeting her with a quick kiss that both surprised and delighted her. "Hey there, gorgeous. You look amazing, but I'm afraid I'm going to have to send you back upstairs to change."

She bit her lower lip. "Not fancy enough?"

"No, too fancy actually. Can you put on a pair of jeans and boots? You'll thank me later." He gave her another squeeze and motioned for her to hurry.

"Umm, I haven't got any boots. At least not here."

"Yeah, fancy is kind of her own personal style. Or at least *stuffy* is." Missy giggled when Louise kicked at the leg of her stool.

"Well, all right then," Brady said with a laugh. "Honest, it's no problem. We'll drop in downtown and pick you up a pair."

"Shopping without me?" Missy teased without shifting her gaze from the computer. "Jealous!"

Louise jogged back up the stairs and changed into a pair of dark wash jeans and sneakers. She also grabbed a cardigan in case the night turned cold. You never knew with this state.

"Have fun tonight," Missy said as Louise and Brady finally left for their date.

Louise waved over her head as Brady ushered her through the front door.

"So, you've got me curious, what are we doing tonight?" Louise asked as she climbed into the cab of

Brady's Ford F350. The rosary dangling from his rearview mirror surprised her, but she chose not to mention it.

He turned the key in the ignition and shot her an adventurous smile. "Riding."

Louise tried not to let her nervousness show. "Riding? Oh, it's been *forever*. I'm not sure I remember how."

"You'll be fine. It's like, well... it's like riding a bike. It'll come back to you."

Kind of like how the whole Anchorage experience had been coming back to her ever since she'd first stepped into town—the way people always smiled and waved when passing her on the street even though she was nothing more than a stranger to most of them, the way the stars took over the entire sky at night leaving her with such a sense of peace and security, and most of all, the way she felt so alive in Brady's company.

A few short minutes into their drive, they stopped at the tanner's shop and picked up a pair of maroon cowboy boots embellished with elaborate stitching for Louise to wear on their ride, and for her to "remember him by."

They were beautiful, but she had no idea what use she'd get out of them in the city. She'd somehow find a way to work them into her wardrobe. She had to. It was only right, considering Brady had insisted on paying the two-hundred-plus price tag since the date had been his idea.

And she loved that he had.

Somehow, he'd managed to take charge in a way that made her feel cherished rather than shoehorned into a submissive role. The city boys back home could learn a thing or two from this small-town gentleman.

Back at the truck, he opened the door for her then drove them another half hour before they reached their destination. Brady parked the car at a large stable off a dirt road. Little purple flowers and flat, smooth pebbles peppered the walkway into the gated area.

The varied smells of pure nature greeted them as they traipsed toward the large wooden building at the other end of the lot. The more Brady showed her of his Alaska, the more she was beginning to think she'd been wrong about it—and about him. Had she somehow repressed all the amazing memories and replaced them with distorted ones as her way of getting over what she'd left behind? That wasn't fair to Brady, and it wasn't fair to herself.

Brady placed a hand on the small of her back as he led her into the gated area outside the structure. "My buddy's letting us borrow a pair of his horses tonight, so we can do a sunset ride. It's the best time of day for one, sunset. After that, we'll go grab some dinner."

"Sounds perfect," Louise said, hitching the gate behind her. And she meant it. She couldn't have asked for a more perfect—or more romantic—night out, least of all with Brady Rockwell, the boy who had always been more wild than thoughtful. What a man he'd become.

"These are our two mounts for the night." Brady walked up to a pair of horses at the far end of the stables. One was black, and the other white with brown spots. A paint, she seemed to remember, it was called.

"They're good horses," Brady said.

Louise tiptoed up to the smaller of the two animals and patted it between its large, gentle eyes. It had been a long time since she'd found herself around animals, and she didn't want to spook the gentle-looking creature by moving too abruptly. Although she'd chosen not to add a pet to her tiny city loft, she'd always liked the idea of one day welcoming an animal companion into her life. Too bad a horse would never work out in the city.

She remembered the rides from her school days so fondly, especially the ones with Brady. He'd taught her the joys of riding, and she'd taught him all about how a good book could transport you to other worlds entirely.

Why had she not thought of either of these things until now? How much had she forgotten about the beauty of simple living?

"Her name's Star," Brady said from behind her as he slipped a saddle on the mare's back. "This one's Sky." He motioned toward the large, black colt beside her.

The horse whinnied and shook his mane, and Brady laughed.

"He's a little unpredictable, so you'll probably do better with Star."

"I think you're right about that." Louise laughed, too, and Star nudged her affectionately with her soft, brown nose.

"See, best friends already." Brady smiled at her, taking a moment to hold her gaze, then shook his head and said, "Let's go, so we can reach the cliffs before the sun goes down."

He swung forward, wrapped his strong hands around her hips, and hoisted her up onto the back of her horse. His touch took her by surprise, mostly for how natural and inviting it felt.

She wished they could have lingered a little longer before heading out on the horses—but she also loved that he had devised such a romantic outing for the two of them. That he knew exactly how to take charge, so she could relax and enjoy the evening.

Louise settled herself into the saddle, as Brady effortlessly pulled himself up by the stirrup and then swung his leg over the other horse to mount.

"Ready?" he asked, his deep eyes hidden by the brim of his hat and the descending night. He steered his horse forward and turned himself around, then walked it back toward Louise and stepped so close their ankles touched.

"Mind if I sneak a quick kiss first? You're just so unbelievably cute. I don't think I can wait until we're through here. Best to clear the air after last night and all, so we can focus on our ride. Besides, I've been waiting fifteen very long years for the chance to kiss you again."

She gulped and nodded with a smile, so he leaned in and took his kiss. It was quick and short—their awkward positions wouldn't allow for much more—but it told of even better things to come. As much as she looked forward to their sunset ride, she also couldn't wait for it to be over.

∾

*a*fter offering a quick riding refresher for Louise, Brady steered his colt toward the worn path on the other side of the stables. Star knew to follow, but Louise wanted to lead.

"*Hyah*," she called, pressing into the mare's ribs with her heel.

Brady watched in astonishment as she pulled ahead on the path. Her form and control were both fantastic, as if she'd been riding regularly for the past ten years.

"Where are we going?" she asked, peeking back at him over her shoulder and scrunching up her nose in an adorable smile that reminded him very much of their younger days.

"Follow the incline." He gestured toward the right, then watched as she sped Star into first a trot, then a gallop.

"Well, if she wants to turn this into a race, we'll give her a run for her money." He patted Sky on the neck and then set him into a full gallop. As he passed Louise, he took in her expression of pure bliss and fell for her even harder than he already had. Any woman who could find this much fun in day-to-day living was a woman he wanted by his side. Who'd ever have guessed that Weezy Gordon would turn out to be that woman?

"This is amazing!" she shouted over the rushing wind. "I feel so free!"

"Race me to the top?" he asked, slowing briefly to match her pace.

"*Hyah*," she called again, speeding forward without technically answering his question. Her lithe body bounced as she navigated the land with ease. If she was sore from the saddle, she sure as heck wasn't letting on.

He loved a woman who could take charge. Made life that much more interesting. He clicked his tongue and allowed Sky to reach his full speed as they sprinted toward the top of the cliff.

They soared quickly past beautiful scenery—lush meadows, a quiet lake, the rich oranges and pinks of the setting sun. In no time at all, they had reached their stopping point, Brady arriving just a hair before Louise.

She let out a joyous, full-bellied laugh as he hitched the horses up and helped Louise down onto her own two feet. "I can see why you love it so much. A part of me never wanted to stop."

Her eyes fixed on his lips as she closed the small

distance between them. "Thank you for this," she whispered. "I think I really needed it."

He brushed a stray strand of hair from her face and traced the outline of her cheek with his finger. "Thank *you* for this," he whispered back taking her in a deep embrace of both arms and lips.

This kiss was different than the one they'd shared in elementary school or the brief peck they'd exchanged before their ride. Her mouth explored his with a confidence he found irresistible. And her body squirmed against his—stretching, reaching, melding.

Could it really be that he'd found the perfect girl for him, so many years ago but only just realized it now? Sure seemed that way.

Louise pulled away, taking the sweet taste of her lips with her. She laid her head on his chest, and together they watched the sun make its final descent over the horizon. He was in serious trouble when it came to Louise Gordon.

Good thing he liked to live dangerously.

8

_L_ouise sat close to Brady in the cab of his truck as they drove back toward town, listening to the local country music station over his tinny speakers. He serenaded her with his best Tim McGraw impression, which was actually pretty good. They drove clear past one restaurant after the next, and Louise's stomach growled in protest.

"I've got something much better," he informed her with a twinkle in his eye.

She smiled and snuggled into his side. Anchorage was bringing out such an unusual side of herself, one she'd long since repressed. Back in Manhattan, everything was focused on efficiency, but here she wanted to slow down and enjoy each day—and especially each evening—as it unwound.

She liked striking out into the evening without a tightly planned agenda or longstanding dinner reservations, and she'd all but forgotten how much slower life moved down here.

Could she have been missing out on life by trying to live it so fast back in the city?

Here, she became vibrant, alive—just as she'd been the last time Brady had taken hold of her heart and given it a good, firm squeeze. Maybe this time could be different. She was more confident now, more sure of herself. She knew how to ask for what she wanted and to make sure she got it.

"We're here," he announced, shifting into park behind a couple other cars along the side of the road. They got out and walked toward a tiny, yellow food truck with bold black lettering and a friendly cartoon pig painted across the side. Four picnic tables sat beneath a pop-up trellis, which was covered with dozens of strings of white lights. Higher up, the Northern stars shone their brightest, free from the light pollution of any major city. The whole scene was straight out of a storybook.

"I love it," Louise gasped, taking in the full charm of the setting before her.

"Just wait until you try the food. Much better than anything you'll find in the lower forty-eight."

"Hey, Brady!" the man inside the truck called out from beneath a large, bushy mustache. "Long time no see. I was beginning to worry about you."

Brady smiled and walked forward to shake Jimbo's hand. "Been on the road, I'm afraid. But don't worry, your stuff is still the best I've found."

"And you brought me a new customer, I see. Who might this lovely lady be?"

Louise blushed. She wasn't used to feeling like a princess, and she definitely wasn't used to enjoying being made to feel that way.

Brady slung an arm over her shoulders and pulled her close. "This is Louise Gordon, and she can't wait to try your number three combo." Turning to Louise, he said, "I remember how you always loved chili cheese fries with extra mustard."

Normally she hated it when a man ordered for her, but a quick scan of the menu confirmed he had made the right choice for her. She also found it sweet how he still remembered her favorite order all these years later.

Maybe what happened between them really had been a big misunderstanding. Maybe she finally needed to let it go and to forgive him.

She was still mulling that over as she and Brady chose a table and took their seats. A few minutes later

Jimbo delivered a pair of piping hot pulled pork sandwiches with sodas and chili cheese fries.

It smelled divine.

Louise covered her portion of fries with French's mustard just as she always had and then popped one into her mouth. The dish definitely had a pleasant kick to it. "So good," she gushed between bites. "Do you eat like this every day?"

"Sure do," he drawled, snagging a fry for himself.

"Then how the heck do you look so good?"

"Hey, gotta fuel my workouts somehow. What do you normally eat?"

"Organic this or that, whole grains, veggies. But none of it tastes like this." She filled her mouth with the warm barbecued pork and let out a small moan of pleasure.

Brady reached across the table and used his thumb to wipe away a bit of stray sauce from Louise's cheek.

So tender, so caring.

"Seems like it was time you shook things up a little. Why did you decide to leave Anchorage in the first place?"

"You mean why did my parents decide to leave?" She shrugged. "My dad got a better job offer in New York."

"Then why did you decide to stay away for so long?" His voice sounded far away, almost sad.

"I never really felt like I belonged here." She shrugged again. "The other girls, their interests were so different. I always preferred books to beauty pageants, skyscrapers to oil rigs. Plus, Rosie kind of made my life a living nightmare."

If Brady was troubled by her mention of Rosie, he sure didn't show it.

"Feels like you belong now." He said and reached across the table to rub her hand. "And I always liked you precisely *because* you were different. You're different than all of them, Louise, and I mean that in the best possible way."

She stopped to study him for a moment.

"Just when I think I have you all figured out, you go and flip the script on me again. Next you're going to tell me you have Sunday brunch with your mother every single week."

"Well, not Sunday, but, yeah, I see her at least a couple times a week. I live just a few blocks over from her, so it's easy to stop in for visits."

"This is not the Brady I remember. What happened to the daring rebel who balked at authority?" She laughed, but he seemed to want to keep things serious.

"I'm still a daredevil at heart, but I've grown up, Louise. Learned a few things along the way."

Louise dipped her sandwich in barbecue sauce. "Why do they call you the bad boy of the rodeo?" She wanted to ask so much more, but this question didn't hurt like the others did.

He grimaced. "I was hoping that wouldn't come up." He let out a deep breath before continuing. "I have a reputation with the ladies."

"So not everything changes then." Louise sniffed, but refused to cry. Why did this past hurt still ache so?

"But you've gotta understand, that's only because I've never found someone who's made me want to settle down. Until now, I mean. You are the best thing I've come across in a long while, and I'd hate to let you get away again."

Louise flushed. She loved spending time with him, but how could she ever trust him again—especially if he still paraded about with an endless string of women on his arm?

"You said all this back then, too, but that didn't stop you from—"

Brady held out his hands to stop her from going on. "Look, I know what I did. And there's not a single day I don't regret it, especially now that you're back and I'm realizing what an idiot I was. I should have fought harder for you, and if I could turn back time, believe me, I would. I thought we were starting fresh here, so I could show you how I've changed."

Louise thought this over. Maybe if they both lived in the city things would be different. But she'd only be in Anchorage a few more days, and long-distance relationships always ended horribly.

Besides, they required way more trust than she was willing to afford him just yet. She'd rather cut things short now while everything still felt wonderful rather than losing both him and the memories they'd formed by dragging it out too long.

"Listen, Brady... I really like you, but we live in two totally different worlds. Not to mention thousands of miles apart. Maybe we should just end things here." She frowned.

"Oh no, you're not getting away that easy." He swallowed his food quickly. "Look, I knew what this was from the start. I know you're only here for a few days, but, darn it, if I don't want every single second you're willing to give to me. Come out with me again tomorrow. Let's have another adventure."

"I don't know." She dabbed at her lips with a napkin and pushed the past memories to the back of her brain. "I dragged Missy all the way here, and I've barely seen her. Besides, if I leave her at home again, she's going to drive herself crazy with all her scattered attempts at wedding planning."

"That's no problem. Bring her with us. I guarantee she'll have a good time, too. And, hey, this time you can even wear a dress." His confident smile seemed to say that the matter was not up for debate.

"Well, if you're sure you understand..."

"Positive. Give me what you can, Louise. I promise not to ask for anything more than you're willing to offer."

"Okay, I can do that." The problem was that what Louise wanted to offer and what she was actually able to give Brady were two very different things. She doubted it was any different for him either.

Stop overthinking everything, she chided herself and took another big bite of sandwich. This doesn't have to be complicated...

Just enjoy it while you can.

~

"Are you kidding?" Missy squealed. "I'd love to go out! Where are we going?"

Louise bit her lip. "Actually, I don't know. But I do know we can wear dresses."

"Then I think this calls for a shopping trip." Any excuse to hit the boutiques.

"I'm not sure I have time, what with the office and all that."

"Hey, leave it to me. I'll find you something fabulous. Still a size eight, right?" Missy eyeballed Louise, and then shook her head. "Hmm, I'll try a six, too."

When Louise returned from the office, Missy dropped a flowy blue sundress into her arms.

"Tada! It's your new dress. Isn't it *so* you? And you can wear your new boots, too. Perfect, right?" Missy talked at a million miles per hour, clearly happy for the company. "Oh, and I picked up those gorgeous boots for me, too, so we can be twinsies. Now, come here, and let me do something fun to your hair."

By the time Brady arrived to pick them up for their big evening, Louise was all decked out. Missy had affixed little faux diamonds throughout her hair and curled it into big ringlets that complemented the sharp angles of her face. She'd also done her makeup, insisting upon a smoky eye and muted lip.

Brady's jaw dropped when Louise opened the door to let him inside. "Missy, could you give us a moment please?" he asked, fixing his gaze on Louise and refusing to look away.

Missy slinked off to find her favorite clutch, and

Brady pulled Louise onto his lap on the couch. "You... look... incredible." He punctuated each word with a lingering kiss, pulling away only far enough to whisper them against her lips. "How am I going to keep my head on straight tonight?"

Louise giggled and stole another little kiss for herself.

After far too short a time, Missy reappeared and cleared her throat loudly. "C'mon, you two. While the night is young." She tossed Louise's purse at them and skipped toward the door.

Brady kept his arm around her as they made their way out to the truck, then snuck another kiss when they got stopped by a red light.

Moments later, they pulled up to Jake's Watering Hole.

"Well, now this is familiar," Louise teased, noticing how much more packed the parking lot was that night versus two nights prior. She barely recognized the place. All the tables had been removed, leaving a giant open space. Couples twisted and turned on the dance floor as a local musician played his guitar and sang a ballad up on a makeshift stage.

A waitress placed drinks in each of their hands. "There's more where that came from," she shouted to make herself heard over all the noise. "Just give a holler when you need topped off."

Brady grabbed the beer from Louise's hands and pulled her out onto the dance floor. He spun her into his chest then out again, and she laughed as she twirled around to the tune of some Toby Keith cover.

Naturally, a line of suitors had already begun to form around Missy. "I'm just watching," she said, letting them down easy. "But thanks for asking!"

"Hey, Brady." A handsome blond man slapped Brady on the back. "Where ya been these past few days? Here I thought you'd shipped off on tour again without saying bye."

He shifted his gaze toward Louise, a huge smile blooming across his face. "Oh, I see now. And who might you be?" He took Louise's hand and planted a kiss on it.

"My lady, so watch it!" Brady teased. Instead, he directed his friend toward Missy. "But perhaps you can keep *her* lady company for the night. Sorry to say she's engaged, but I'm sure she'd appreciate any help you can give in getting all these other guys to leave her be."

"Oh, gosh, yes. Please help me." Missy laughed, and he saddled her hand with a kiss, too.

"Name's Stud."

Missy and Louise looked at each other, unsure whether to laugh or say hello to "Stud".

"It's true, that's really his name," Brady said. "Long story. Of course, Stud tells it better than I do."

"Well, actually..." Stud took the bait, and turned to Missy, allowing Brady and Louise to slip away.

The singer headed into a cover of Shania Twain's "You're Still the One", making Louise wonder if he had somehow gotten into her brain.

"How 'bout that?" Brady grinned, pulling her in tight to his chest. They swayed in time to the ballad.

She pressed her cheek into his chest and heard the gentle pitter-patter of his heartbeat. *Safe.* The world slowed. Everything was perfect. At least for that moment.

While secure in Brady's arms, it was okay that she'd been away from her New York office during a crucial period in the search for the firm's new partner. It was okay that they still hadn't made much progress with her aunt's estate here just outside of Anchorage. It was okay that she and Brady came from two different worlds, because they were here and now together in this own world of their own making, in a perfect world, one she didn't want to leave.

Unfortunately, the night would have to end eventually. All the problems of her real life would come flooding back to her. Her head spun as she tried to forget her broken past with Brady and to envision a future for the two of them.

No, it could never work, not in the long term.

But as for now...

She would just keep dancing.

9

The unmistakable intro to "Tequila Makes Her Clothes Fall Off" began, and Brady reluctantly loosened his embrace around Louise. He hated to let go of their slow dance to speed up to the new beat, but was rewarded with the adorably sassy sway of her hips as she let loose.

"Sounds like me, doesn't it?" she joked, and he had to agree.

The night carried on, an irresistible mix of holding Louise close through the ballads and watching her shimmy and shake to the more up-tempo numbers. Forget falling, he had *fallen*— and hard—for this strong, passionate woman. How would he move past her and back into his everyday life?

She bounced her head to the beat, reminding him

of the first time their paths had crossed, way back in the sixth grade. His family had just moved to town from Austin, Texas, and while he missed his hometown friends, he immediately fell in with the popular crowd at Anchorage. He'd only just begun to take notice of girls, of course, but that didn't stop him from asking Rosie Hector to be his girlfriend. After all, she was the girl every boy wanted, and she'd made it very clear that what *she* wanted was Brady.

One night, Rosie threw an innocent enough middle school party with her older sisters chaperoning the whole affair in her parents' basement. And her parents had said that she had to invite everyone so that none of their classmates felt left out.

One such person was Weezy Gordon.

When she walked down the stairs and up to the punch bowl, Rosie's face took on a poisonous expression. He should've known right then and there to stay as far away from Rosie as possible—should've, would've, could've.

"What's *she* doing here?" Rosie groaned. "Yeah, I mean, I invited her because my parents made me, but I didn't think she'd actually show. Some nerve." She placed her hands on her hips and shot daggers toward her unwanted party guest.

Brady looked over the wispy girl in the corner,

amused—and kind of impressed—that she had decided to bring a book with her to a dance party. He wanted to ask her what it was about, but Rosie refused to let him stray more than a few feet from her side the whole night, constantly grumbling a string of complaints about the unpopular girl who had dared to show up at her VIP-only party.

Weezy, however, was clearly not bothered. She alternated between sipping punch while burying her nose in the novel she'd brought and dancing by herself whenever the boom box's oversized speakers blasted out a song she liked.

And she was still that same fearless, intelligent, devil-may-care girl today. She even had some of the same dance moves. Only she was all grown up now. Still as strong as ever, but she'd also developed a softer side; she'd started to allow him back in.

Not like before when she had always placed him second to her ambitions—which at the time was nothing more than maintaining the highest grades in the class. Now she'd achieved her career goals and seemed to have realized there was more she could get out of life.

But he also knew that she would never leave behind the life she'd worked so hard for, least of all to take a chance on him. He still hadn't regained her trust—he understood that. He had a lot of making up to do if he expected her to truly let him back in.

At the same time, he had no idea what kind of life would await him in New York City, or even if he'd be welcomed there. It wasn't as if rodeo jobs fell from the sky. He'd worked diligently, too. Why did he have to fall for a girl who lived clear across the country, and why so hard?

Another slow song started up and Louise burrowed into his arms. She felt so good there, like it was exactly where she had always belonged. They kissed, sparking another memory from way back when.

Rosie had called it quits on Brady shortly after that disaster of a party. Apparently, he wasn't invested in their relationship, or, in other words, he didn't fawn over her quite enough for her liking.

Well, that was fine by him. He hadn't liked her much anyway.

And even though he'd escaped Rosie's grasp, Weezy had never quite been able to get away. The two girls bickered mercilessly, and he knew which one of them was to blame, too.

One day, he'd had to stay late after school to serve detention—something to do with spitballs—and his mom was late in picking him up. Brady wandered around the playground kicking at stones and trying to keep himself busy. He'd thought he was all alone, but then a flutter of movement near the kickball court caught his eye.

"What are you doing here so late?" Weezy demanded, holding her thumb inside her book to mark the page she'd been reading.

"Detention."

"Figures." She rolled her eyes.

"How about you?" he asked hoping to strike up a conversation and get to know her a little better. It was easier without the noisy heckling of his buddies, and he didn't want to waste the opportunity to be one-on-one with her.

"I live nearby, and I like to come here sometimes after everyone is gone. It's like a whole other place when it's empty, you know." She kept her eyes fixed on the ground as she spoke to him. "Why are you talking to me anyway? Rosie won't like it."

"We broke up." He gestured toward her book. "Tell me. What are you reading?"

"This?" She lifted up her book and showed him the cover. "*Little Women*. It's my favorite."

"What's it about?"

Apparently, he'd struck upon the right conversation starter, because Louise launched into a passionate retelling of the book she so loved.

Her eyes lit with a fire he hadn't often seen, especially in his peers. She laughed when she told him of Amy's childish antics and became somber when she discussed Beth. Brady felt like he was living in the story himself. Her passion was inspiring, but most of all it was incredibly beautiful.

He stopped her when she paused to take a breath amidst her discussion of Laurie and his various romantic endeavors. "Could I kiss you?"

Her eyes grew wide and she swallowed hard, when just seconds earlier she'd been talking freely and easily. "What? What about Rosie?"

"I told you we broke up. And now I'd really like to kiss *you*. May I?"

She didn't say anything for a long time, and he'd worried he'd lost any chance he may have had by being too abrupt, but then she slowly nodded and said, "Okay."

He leaned forward awkwardly and pressed his mouth to his. He hadn't kissed anyone before, but he'd seen lots of such kisses in the movies. He tipped his head to the right and parted her lips with his tongue, consuming her like a fine beverage.

He drank that moment in, drank her in that day—
and he'd never quite been able to shake her since.

~

*L*ouise woke up in a wonderful mood. Things
were moving ahead both with Brady and with
Aunt Maddie's estate. In fact, today would be
the day they finally read her will.

Around noon, the few remaining Gordon relatives
arrived along with a number of key people from
around Anchorage and charity representatives from
the state. Her father hadn't been able to make the trip
from New York, and she didn't know anyone else in
the room, which made it easy to handle this estate like
any other. Not that there had been many others.

She ran through each item, reading out what her
aunt had bequeathed to whom and under what conditions. "To the Make-A-Wish Foundation, I leave fifty
thousand dollars," she read. "To be used expressly to
aid in the wishes of children with cancer and from the
state of Alaska."

As long as no one contested the will—and she
didn't see why they would, given Aunt Maddie's
amazing generosity—she'd be free and clear to return
to New York tomorrow morning.

The managing partner of her firm back home had called earlier that morning to request a meeting with her when she returned. From the sound of his voice, it seemed more good news was in store for Louise. The only piece that didn't factor in perfectly to the good things that lay ahead was Brady.

But then again, he had never fit well in her life anyway.

"To my second cousin, Ruth, I leave my farm in Iowa, provided she promises to continue growing a minimum of ten rows of corn each harvest."

What kinds of conditions would she and Brady need to tack onto their relationship to make things work?

To Brady, I promise my love and devotion, provided you visit me in New York at least two weekends per month and call me no less than four times per week?

The whole prospect was ridiculous and not one she wanted to entertain for a second longer.

She'd walked away from him before. Would she have to do that again so they could both freely pursue their careers?

"To my niece, Louise, I leave my ranch, provided she is willing to live there at least fifty percent of the year. If these conditions prove disagreeable, she is to oversee the sale of the property and donate all proceeds from the sale to The Make-A-Wish Foundation following the same stipulations cited above."

Louise stopped reading and looked around the room. She wasn't the only one who seemed shocked by this particular bequeathal.

A hundred-thousand thoughts raced through her mind—Why her? Why this property? Would her parents be too terribly disappointed if she turned down the generous gift?—but she pushed them all back in order to continue through the reading.

"And lastly, to my good friend Sara, I leave my remaining monetary assets to be used to promote her campaign for governor and hopefully one day for president." Louise glanced up. Another surprise about her late aunt. How well had she even known her at all? Of course, it was no surprise that the politician had not made an appearance for the reading. She'd need to get her people on the phone to round out this item.

"Well, thank you kindly, for coming out today," Bill Ringstead said as he ushered everyone out of the office. "Louise and I will be in touch over the next week. You know how to find me, if you need me."

When they had all departed, he turned to Louise with a big smile on his face. "I'll bet that was a surprise!"

"Definitely was." Louise returned his smile, but still

wasn't sure how she felt about this latest turn of events.

"That explains why she insisted it be you who handled her estate. Suppose that's the only way she figured she'd get you out here. Anyway, the place is gorgeous. I'm sure you'll be very happy there. That is, if you decide to stay." He bent down toward his safe and extracted a dangling set of keys. "These are yours now. Do you know where you're going?"

Louise nodded. "Thank you, Bill. I do."

"Why don't you head out early and go take a look? We've got everything handled around here. I'll email you our progress a bit later."

Louise eagerly accepted Bill's offer and headed home to grab Missy, so they could both check out the property together.

"I can't believe your aunt left you her house. That's crazy!" her friend squealed, apparently much more excited about this than Louise herself.

"Yeah, it's too bad I can't pick the whole thing up and move it to Manhattan."

"Can't you keep it as a vacation home or something?"

"Would that I could, but there's no getting around the fifty percent residency stipulation, and it's not like lawyers can work from home, especially when their core client base is in New York City."

"Yeah, that's a problem. So, what happens then, if you don't take it?"

"It's not *if*, Missy. There's no way I can accept this." She sighed as the realization struck her. "I have to sell it and then the proceeds will go to the Make-A-Wish Foundation."

"Well, that's good at least. Kind of sucks though, to receive a huge gift like this and then ending up having to do extra work to get rid of it. I'm sorry, Weezy." She reached over for a hug.

Louise didn't even bother to tell Missy again not to call her by the hated nickname. They'd be leaving soon enough, and this whole thing would be behind them.

For better or for worse.

They stopped driving as they neared the edge of town. Her aunt's—actually, *her*—ranch lay sprawled across a gorgeous meadow, much like where Brady had taken her for their ride. Her heart skipped a beat when she spied the large stables near the back of the property. It had space for several horses, and hadn't she always wanted her own horse?

The home itself was beautiful and only in slight disrepair. It looked as if it hadn't been updated either since the mid-sixties, which was a problem that would need to be addressed... but by the next owner of the home.

This wasn't hers. She was just passing through.

They tiptoed through the house and out onto the sunroom. The space would be perfect for her desk. She could take her coffee and files here while watching the sunrise from the comfort of her own home. Her aunt had even planted a garden of beautiful blooms right outside the massive window. She could add her own organic veggies to the mix. She'd always wanted to grow her own, but had never had the space in her tiny Manhattan window box....

And she still didn't. This wasn't hers. Not really.

"It's too bad you can't keep it," Missy mumbled. "It's really beautiful."

"Yeah," Louise admitted. "I know."

She turned away from the sunroom then marched through the living room and out the front door. "Let's get out of here. The longer we stay, the harder it will be to leave, "she said, knowing she wasn't just talking about the ranch.

Her time in Anchorage was up, and she needed to get out of there while she still had the nerve.

---

10

*A*fter he got done with chores around his mother's house, Brady decided to swing by Louise's place. Even though it was already evening, neither of the girls were anywhere to be found. All the lights in the house were off and even the driveway sat empty—no truck.

Had they really left without saying goodbye? Had Louise decided she was done with him once and for all?

Fear gnawed at him. "I'll come by again in the morning," he told the empty house before driving away, then ventured over to Jake's Watering Hole, had his usual.

"Why so down?" Shelby asked, sliding a bottle of Kicker Session his way.

Brady shrugged and tore at the label on his beer.

"What happened to your lady friend?"

He took off his hat and scratched his head. "I'm not sure, actually."

"You two seemed really good together. I hope everything's all right," Shelby offered him a kind smile before making her way over to a new group of customers who had just sat down.

He sure was glad he and Shelby had managed to stay friends after their brief attempt at a relationship a few years back. Shelby always knew exactly what to say to help smooth things over.

Too bad they lacked any real chemistry.

Still, maybe things would have been simpler if he'd hung on to Shelby a bit harder. Because, at the end of the day, wasn't friendship the basis for the best relationships?

Louise excited him, but she also frustrated him.

Their differences were both arousing and annoying. Not only did she have a hard time trusting him, but now she'd managed to disappear without giving him a heads-up? Had she decided that she couldn't get past what Rosie had done to her—to them—way back when?

Sigh. He'd been such a moron, letting Rosie back into his head.

At the beginning of their sophomore year, things went off track. Louise had really blossomed over the summer, picking up curves in all the right places and attracting Brady more than ever. Of course, his buddies gave him loads of grief for it.

Louise is off limits—nothing more than a book geek. He should set his sights higher. Rosie is single again.

Still, he ignored all their warnings and decided to ask Louise to homecoming. After a few days' hesitation, she agreed, and he was over the moon planning how to make that night special. Of course, thanks to Rosie, they never got their chance to make that memory.

Rosie spread vicious rumors throughout the school that Weezy had given it up to him in exchange for a date to the dance—because why else would a guy ever want to be seen with *her*? And her rumors traveled far and fast. When the queen bee wanted to buzz, everyone stopped to listen.

Brady had insisted that it wasn't true, that he genuinely liked Louise and always had, but his buddies gave him a never-ending stream of high fives to congratulate him on the score.

"So, what is she like? A naughty librarian? Super hot!"

"Who knew such a freak was hiding behind all those books?"

"You think I could have a go at her when you're through, man?"

He tried to hush his friends, to tell them to back off, but it was too late. Rosie had far more power over the social scene than he did, and she refused to back down.

Weezy tromped up to him with giant tears glistening in her normally bright eyes. "How could you?" she demanded.

His friends' roaring laughter drowned out his attempts to speak, and Louise ran away before he could even so much as apologize.

He followed her to her house after school and tried his best to make up with her, but she wouldn't have it. He tried for weeks, months, before he found out she'd be moving clear across the country. And he'd caught up with her right before the cab took her to the airport and away forever, but she hadn't been willing to hear him out. She'd just said goodbye and moved on with her life, like what they had together hadn't even mattered.

But she had mattered a great deal to him. He was sure of it now just as sure as he was then.

She was the first girl he'd ever really loved. But it

all got thrown away because of one jealous ex and one stupid rumor. The fact that she was hurting tore him up inside, but then again, no one would believe him when he said it wasn't true. He wished that she'd at least believed him. He'd thought she knew him better than that.

Even now all these years later, it seemed like she was still waiting for the other shoe to drop. How could he convince her that it wouldn't? Was it even worth trying? He liked a challenge, but at a certain point enough was enough already.

"Doing okay over here?" Shelby leaned over the bar, placed a hand on his shoulder, and smiled. She always had a smile for him, no matter how bad things got. He liked that.

But he wasn't sure he had an answer to her question. Should he let Louise go once and for all? Maybe try an easier route—reignite things with Shelby? Or should he fight for her—for them—even if that meant flying to New York to make sure they at least got a proper goodbye?

He glanced up. Shelby really was beautiful with her white-blonde hair and sparkling green eyes, and a true class act besides.

But she wasn't Louise, wasn't *his* Louise.

"Everything's fine, but I best be off. Good evenin' to

you." He tipped his hat and slapped a twenty onto the bar. He'd never get Louise off his brain until he at least got some answers. They were good together, almost too good to be true. And he refused to give up without a fight.

He was going in, ready to lay it all bare, hoping for the best.

$\sim$

*H*e drove by her place again and—lucky break—she and Missy were just pulling into the gravel driveway.

"Brady, hi." She gave him a quick hug, but her face fell as she pulled away, concern swimming in her eyes. "What's wrong?"

"Nothing, now that you're here." He smiled but kicked himself for being so sappy.

"What's up?"

He took off his hat and placed it on his chest. "Come out with me again tonight."

"Brady, I... We closed up the estate today. Missy and I will be flying back to New York tomorrow." She shifted her weight to her other foot and looked down at his boots.

"Then all the more reason to give me tonight," he

insisted. "Tell me, have you had dinner yet?"

She sighed. "No, but—"

"Good, I know a great little place. C'mon, let's go."

Louise whispered an apology to Missy, but Missy shook her off. "Are you kidding me? Go, go! We'll catch up on the plane, right?"

She headed toward his truck, but then stopped. "Maybe I should change first."

"No, you're perfect just as you are." Brady opened the passenger door for her and kissed her as she slipped past him.

"Where are we going anyway?" she asked, buckling her seatbelt.

"You'll see." He smiled as he backed out of the driveway and turned onto the main road. "It's a bit of a drive, so get comfortable. Figured we could talk along the way."

Louise smiled, too, and poked at his swinging rosary. "And you're sure you won't tell me where we're headed?"

"Nope, it'll be more fun as a surprise."

"Okay, then can I ask a question?"

"Shoot." He attempted to smile, but he had a feeling that the same shared moment from their past was on her mind, too.

Sure enough, she licked her lips and asked, "Why

did you help Rosie spread that rumor about me back in high school?"

He tried not to frown, but couldn't help it. "Going straight for the hard stuff, hey?"

"It's my last night here. Figured it was about time I got some closure, since I never had the chance to get it back then."

"Very well then. If I tell you, do you promise to believe me?"

"Present the evidence first, and then I'll decide." Louise rolled down the window, then crossed her arms over her chest.

"Well then, Judge Gordon, I plead not guilty." He glanced at her from the corner of his eye and found that she was wearing a scowl.

"But I saw you talking with your friends, remember? Surely you can't deny what I heard with my own two ears?"

"Did you ever actually hear me say that though? Because I didn't." He'd said all these words back then, too, but she'd refused to trust him. Would she see things differently this time?

Her eyes glistened. "But was it true? Did you ask me to the dance just because you thought I would…" She trailed off and took a deep breath before continuing. "That you thought I'd sleep with you?"

He wished they could have this conversation anywhere but here. He needed to be able to hold her, to look into her eyes, to reassure her he was telling the truth. "Louise, you've never been some conquest for me. You weren't then, and you aren't now. I mean, look, I knew you were just in town for a few days, but did I ever try to put the moves on you?"

She played with some loose stitching on the edge of her seatbelt. "No, but—"

"No, I didn't. Because you aren't just some random date to me, Louise. I care about you so much more than that. I thought you knew."

"But, back then, I mean. You were a teenage guy, I get it." She fiddled with the air conditioning controls, twisting them back and forth as she talked. "You just have no idea how hard that made things for me after the rumor got started."

He wanted so badly to reach out and touch her, to assure her of his intentions with a bit of physical comfort, but that seemed out of place here. All they had for the moment were words. He hoped his were enough.

"I tried to stop it. I really did. I told them all it wasn't true, but no one believed me."

She huffed, looking straight at him again. "You could have tried harder to defend my honor."

"Yes, I could've, and I wish I had. I'd fight for you now though, except I promised not to force you into anything more than you wanted."

She looked out the window, making her voice seemed far away. "Thank you for that."

"Let me just say that I'd love the chance to turn this into something real, if you're willing to give me that chance. The decision is up to you." He pushed his hand across the seat and laced his fingers with hers.

"Brady..." She shook him off and crossed her arms again. "I leave tomorrow."

"So? There is such a thing as the telephone—and planes."

She groaned. "Long distance? I don't think so."

"Why not?" He took a chance and shifted his gaze from the road ahead to the beautiful woman beside him. "You never gave me the chance back then. Give me the chance now."

She motioned back toward the road and frowned. "You said you wouldn't pressure me."

"And I won't. That's the last I'll say on the matter, but I wanted to be sure you knew how I felt, what I'm willing to offer, should you choose to accept."

"Okay." From her tone, he couldn't tell whether she'd taken him seriously, whether she'd chosen to believe him this time. But he had told the truth, and that had to count for something.

"Okay."

Louise reached over to turn on the radio. "Now will you tell me where we're going?"

He laughed, thankful for the change of topic. "Ha, nice try."

"You're a tough nut to crack, Rockwell." She reached over and took his hand, giving it a firm squeeze.

"I know. Mind if I ask a question now?"

"That only seems fair."

"Why don't you like it when I call you Weezy anymore?"

She frowned again, and the cab grew hot with tension. "You seriously don't know?"

"I seriously don't."

She scrunched up her face and sang, "*Weezy, Weezy. So, so easy.*"

"What?"

"You can't honestly tell me that's the first time you heard that?"

He shook his head, completely baffled.

"How is it that I heard that every day of my life while I lived in Anchorage, and you didn't manage to hear it once?"

"Did Rosie...?" He let his question linger.

"Of course, she did. That rumor destroyed me, you know. Rosie threw condoms at me in the hall to 'protect all the boys from my filth'. Guys constantly tried to push me into the locker room, because I looked like I was 'asking for it'. Even a teacher called me into his classroom after school and tried to put the moves on me. Moving all the way across the country didn't erase any of that hurt. It cut too deep to ever really heal."

Now he felt tears struggling to break free from his own eyes. If he'd have known any of that was going on, he would have fought harder. He would have protected her, no matter what it took, even if it cost him his spot on the football team, even if it got him expelled. "I didn't know how bad it got. I'm so sorry you had to go through that. You certainly didn't deserve any of it."

"No, I didn't, but I do appreciate the apology."

Brady pulled over to the side of the road and stopped the truck. He turned to caress Louise's cheek, making sure she looked into his eyes as he spoke. "You are more than your past, okay? You are a brilliant, strong, amazing—and, yes, beautiful—woman. You have so much more to offer than what they said. You are the complete package, Louise. Whichever guy gets you in the end is the luckiest man alive, and I for one hope he's me."

He leaned in to kiss her, and she accepted. They sat there for a while, just enjoying each other as they gained some distance from the painful memories they'd just relived.

She offered a sad smile and ran her index finger across his lower lip. "*Now* will you tell me where we're going?"

He laughed. "Will it make you feel better?"

"Yes."

"Okay then, but just remember, I wanted it to be a surprise."

"Okay, so dish." She put her seatbelt back on and straightened her posture.

"We're going to the Frosty Peak in Fairbanks."

"Wait, *the* Fairbanks?"

"It's the only one I know."

"But why drive so far? Isn't it like six hours away?" Her features arranged themselves into a quizzical expression.

A smile slowly stretched across Brady's face. "Six and a half, but maybe that will be enough time to convince you to stay."

He stopped to study her. "Is that okay with you?"

She nodded. "It will be a good way to say goodbye."

He didn't know what to say, so he sang along with Alan Jackson as his twang flooded through the speakers. Louise had finally listened to his side of the story and seemed to have forgiven him, but it also seemed as if she'd already decided to let him go.

11

*L*ouise shoved the last of her toiletries into her suitcase and pulled the zipper closed. Their time here had come and gone so fast, and now she and Missy were leaving. She never would have imagined she'd be sad to go, but what could she do about it now? She needed to get home, and home wasn't here—not anymore.

She pulled on the boots Brady had bought for her, then grabbed a banana and a bottle of water as she and Missy headed out the door.

"Can you believe our five days are already up? It seems like we just landed yesterday, and now we're going home."

"Yeah, I know." Louise looked down the street, half expecting to see Brady—but they had already said their goodbyes early this morning. He'd just dropped her off a few hours ago, in fact. They'd spent the entire night driving to and from Fairbanks so that they could grab dinner at the Frosty Peak and soak in every last moment they had together. It had been a beautiful evening to remember him by, one she wouldn't be forgetting soon, or ever for that matter.

And he'd given her the greatest gift of all—closure. They'd talked through everything that had and hadn't happened all those years ago. They'd been honest with each other and with themselves. It had been the perfect ending to something that never really got the chance to begin.

Because now real life was calling.

She had a meeting with her boss and the partners the next morning and would have to cram in at least eight hours of work on the Kleinmann case before then. Not to mention, checking in with her neighbor to collect her mail, going to the store to restock her fridge, and somehow finding a way to adjust herself back to East Coast time. Maybe she should get a cat to keep her company—now that her time with Brady had reminded her how much she loved having animals in her life. She'd have to do her research on that as well.

Thinking of all she needed to do made her tired,

and not just because she hadn't managed to grab much shut-eye the night before. Now that she'd taken a few days to slow down, she didn't know if she was quite ready to speed up again.

She and Missy stopped by the local realtor's office to drop off the key to Aunt Maddie's ranch. Another shame.

Sure, Brady had given her closure on their past, but a whole new crop of regrets had sprouted up during her brief stay in Anchorage.

It's for charity, she reminded herself. It would be selfish to keep it. Aunt Maddie couldn't have expected I'd stay.

"I feel like I understand you a little better, now that I've seen where you come from," Missy said as they rolled through the mountain-lined streets one last time.

"Me, too." And she really did. She'd discovered parts of herself that she'd long since forgotten. Burying the bad memories also meant forgetting the good. And this trip had reminded her of both sets. It had reintroduced her to who she had been so many years ago, who she still was deep down on the inside.

"Was it weird coming back so many years later?" Missy asked.

"Yeah, but a good weird, I think."

They drove in silence for a few minutes as both looked out at the scenery that flew by the windows.

"What will you do when you get back?"

"Work."

Missy slumped back in her seat and looked out the window. "Figured."

"How about you?"

She smiled, but she didn't seem happy. "Jordan."

"Yeah."

Several more minutes passed.

"Missy?"

"Yeah?"

"What's wrong? Are you mad at me for abandoning you all week? I feel horrible."

She sighed. "No, it's not that."

"Then what?" Louise drummed her fingers on the steering wheel while she waited for her friend to work out an answer.

"It's just... I thought... well, I just really thought you and Brady were going to work things out."

"Why?"

She shrugged. "I don't know exactly. You just seemed right. I thought things were supposed to work out no matter what when they were right."

Louise grimaced. Leaving Brady behind was hard enough already; she didn't need Missy throwing it back in her face before they'd hardly had a chance to make it out of town. "Maybe for you and Jordan they did, but we can't all be so lucky."

"Maybe."

Still, her friend seemed genuinely upset.

"Hey, chin up. I'm fine. You should be fine, too."

"Maybe I just need a distraction. Mind if I drive?"

"It's a stick shift, remember?"

Missy frowned. "I know. I—I kind of lied about not being able to drive one."

"Why would you do that?" Louise turned to study Missy. Lying was not like her at all.

"So that you would give Brady a chance. It was just a feeling I had. Clearly, I was wrong. I'm so sorry, Weezy—I mean, Louise."

She relaxed her grip on the steering wheel, noticing her knuckles had started to turn white. In a way, what Missy had tried to do for her was sweet. "It's okay, you can call me that. I don't mind it anymore. And, thank you, I'm glad you pushed us together. It helped me sort out a few important things."

"But you're not together."

"So what? Relationships don't have to last forever to be special. Maybe Brady and I already got what we needed." Even as she said the words, she knew she didn't believe them. She doubted Missy would either.

"Maybe we're ready to move on to bigger and better things now. Maybe my prince charming is already waiting for me in Manhattan. You never know, right?"

Missy shifted toward the door, leaning away from Louise in a way that felt like an insult. "I guess."

"Missy, seriously, can you please stop? Leaving is hard enough already, and you're kind of making things harder."

"Because he's right for you, and you know it, too."

"Can we please talk about something else? Anything?"

"Fine. Tell me about your big meeting tomorrow," Missy said, but Louise noticed she had tears welling up behind her eyes.

They chatted idly as they finished their drive to the airport, but Louise didn't have her heart in it. The whole confrontation was so unlike Missy, she had to stop and wonder if she'd been too hasty in saying goodbye to Brady. Did Missy know something she didn't? If so, what?

Actually, what did it matter? She'd already made her decision. They both had. And it was too late to change it. She'd lived the last dozen years without Brady; she could easily move forward without him again.

When Missy disappeared into her phone, Louise let her. It was hard being alone with her thoughts, but it was even harder feeling like her best friend disapproved of a decision that she had no choice but to make.

They returned their truck to the rental shop and then took a shuttle to the main terminal. As they waited in line to check their baggage, Missy continued to type furiously on her phone.

"What's up?" Louise asked. Missy wasn't usually much of a texter.

"Jordan. Making plans for tonight. Sorry, I'll just be a few more seconds."

"Hey, don't worry about it." She took out her own phone and scrolled through her work emails. At least ten more regarding the Kleinmann case had arrived since she'd last checked. It was going to be a very long night, indeed.

The line moved forward, and Louise placed her phone into her briefcase. When she looked back at Missy, her friend was wearing a huge smile.

"I knew he'd make it!" Missy wrapped her arms around Louise and turned her to look in the opposite direction. "I told you it wasn't over! Look!"

Brady rushed forward, carrying a bouquet of wildflowers and a small, shiny gift bag in his hands.

Louise looked from Brady to Missy. "What's going on?"

"What's going on is that you get your own happily ever after, Louise. He came for you."

"But—"

"But nothing, you have to talk to him. Go!" She pushed Louise out of the line, then whispered, "Good luck."

Luck? Did luck really have anything to do with what happened in their lives? Louise had worked hard for everything she had. She'd fought for it. To say things came down to luck was insulting.

No, luck couldn't make your success, but it could certainly unmake it. She and Brady had been plagued by one stroke of bad luck after another.

It had been bad luck that Rosie had taken up such a hatred for her, especially when Louise had never done a single thing to hurt her. And it had been bad luck that Rosie had maintained that hatred for years, deciding to spread that rumor just as she and Brady were about to give things another try in high school. It had been bad luck that her dad had taken a new job across the country before she could decide whether she wanted to give him another chance.

And it was bad luck now that neither of their careers was transportable, that they had no real way of making things work when they so clearly wanted to be with each other.

She watched Brady as he wove between the endless streams of travelers and made his way over to her. A huge grin lit up his handsome face.

"These are for you," he said, placing the flowers into the crook of her arm.

"Brady, what are you doing here? I thought—"

"I know I said I wouldn't ask for more than you could give, but I just couldn't let you get away again. I couldn't."

He bent down to kiss her, and all the feelings she'd convinced herself she'd put to rest came rushing back.

Reluctantly, she shook off his embrace and turned toward the ticket counter. "Brady, my flight... I have to go."

"I know, but not without letting me give you this first." He placed the gift bag in her empty hand.

"What is it?" She peered at him, unsure.

But he only greeted her with a childlike smile, every bit as excited as he'd been the first time he'd asked to kiss her on the playground. "Open it and see."

She pulled a very old dog-eared paperback book from the bag. *Little Women*. Her favorite book.

"How did you...?"

He took the book from her and thumbed through

it to show her all the notes he had taken in the margins. "I picked it up years ago. When you told me about it that day, I knew I had to read it for myself. And I've read it many times since then. I always thought we were a lot like Laurie and Jo."

"But Laurie and Jo don't end up together."

"Yeah, but I always thought they should have."

Louise shook her head and looked away. "Brady, I can't."

"Just promise me you'll think it over. Can you do that?"

Just think it over. There was nothing *just* about it. She'd been wracking her brain the whole way to the airport, trying to think of some scenario that would allow them to be together, but there weren't any. They lived in two different worlds. She couldn't give up all she'd worked so hard for, especially not when she was so close to achieving partnership status.

"Thank you for coming to say goodbye." She gave Brady a long hug, then turned around and headed toward the security check with Missy stumbling behind her.

12

*L*ouise walked down the narrow aisle of the plane. She couldn't believe she was actually going through with this, but she also knew that she needed to go forward with no regrets, no second thoughts. She jammed her carry-on into the overhead bin and smiled at the person occupying the window seat next to her.

"An eight-hour flight. Please tell me you have an interesting story to tell. By the way, I'm Claire," the woman said, offering Louise a candy from her box of Good n' Plenty.

Louise held out her hand to accept the candy and smiled at the kind stranger. "I'm Louise. And as a matter of fact..."

The plane sped up down the runway and lifted

into the sky. Louise had thought long and hard about all that happened with Brady, and she finally felt ready to put it into words.

So, she told the old woman the story of her big return to Anchorage, of running into Brady again, of their amazing night *en route* to and from Fairbanks. Claire's attention never wavered as Louise went into all the details of how her story had unfolded. When Louise told her about how Brady had caught up with her at the airport, Claire's eyes glistened with intrigue.

"And then what happened? Did you get on the plane?"

Louise nodded, and Claire let out a gasp of horror. "I did."

"After all that you two didn't even end up together? No offense, but that's a terrible story."

"Well...." Louise smiled. "I didn't say it was over."

She clapped her hands lightly against one another. "Oh, goodie. Please do continue."

"I got on the plane and went back to New York. I worked through the night to catch up on my case, and went to my law office the next morning to meet with the partners."

"And?" Her eyes were wide as she waited for Louise to continue.

"And I was right, they did offer me the new partner

position." She accepted another candy from Claire's outstretched palm. This time it was a Twizzler.

"Oh, that's wonderful."

Louise shook her head as she chewed. "I thought it would be, but when they offered it, I realized I didn't want it. Not really." Her whole life she had been working hard to get ahead, and she'd finally made it, but the victory felt hollow.

"So, what did you do?"

A huge smile took over Louise's face. "I quit, right then and there."

"You didn't?" She gasped again. "Oh, I bet your bosses weren't pleased."

"They weren't. In fact, they even told me that old cliché, you know the one. *You'll never work in this town again.* So, I said fine. I'm through with this town anyway."

"And your fella?"

"Will be pleasantly surprised when I show up at his door tonight."

"You mean he doesn't—?"

"Nope."

"Oh, that's so terribly romantic. But, tell me, what are you going to do for work?"

"That's easy. I'm going to follow my dreams, my real ones. Coming back to my hometown reminded me of who I was *before* I became a big shot city lawyer."

"And who might that be, dear?"

Louise held up the dog-eared copy of *Little Women* that rested upon her lap. "I was a girl who more than anything else loved to read."

Claire squealed. "Oh, are you going to write your story?"

"No, I still love the law, but I don't love the corporate stuff I've been doing. I'm going to start my own practice to help authors and publishers navigate their literary rights."

"In Anchorage?"

"With frequent trips back to New York. My friend Missy's agreed to let me crash at her place whenever I need to."

"That sounds perfect," Claire said, rubbing Louise on the shoulder.

Louise nodded. "Even more perfect is the fact that Bill Ringstead offered me part-time work at his office in Anchorage. That way there's no pressure for me to make it or break it right away. I can take my time, do things right."

"And you'll have your aunt's ranch?"

"I will, and I'm planning to get a couple horses of my own, too."

"Now isn't that just lovely? I do wish you the best, dear."

The captain's raspy voice came on over the airplane's speakers. "We're now making our final descent into Anchorage. Should be just a few more moments here, folks."

"Would you look at that? With you to keep me company, it was like no time had passed at all. Thank you for telling me your story. It's a good one."

Louise laughed. "Yes, I think so, too."

They both rose to collect their luggage from the overhead bins, and while they waited for the passengers in front of them to get a move on, Claire turned to Louise once again. "By the way, my daughter is an author, and, well, she could use a good person like you in her corner. Here's her card. I'll let her know you'll be in touch."

When Louise saw the name that was printed in bold across the white business card, her eyes popped. Maybe there was such a thing as good luck, after all. "Your daughter's...?" she asked, unable to believe that she'd just met and spent an enjoyable afternoon with one of her favorite author's mothers.

The old woman beamed with pride. "None other. Goodbye now, dear."

Louise really couldn't believe her good luck. She

hadn't even officially started her own practice yet, and already she had a lead on a mega bestselling client. She felt like she was floating as she exited first the plane, then the airport, then the expressway on her way to Anchorage.

~

She found Brady at Jake's Watering Hole, sitting by himself at the bar.

"Why, hello, good lookin'," she drawled, taking a seat beside him.

"*You*." His breath seemed to catch in his throat as he looked her up and down, almost as if he couldn't believe she was real.

Louise wore what must have been the biggest smile of her entire life. "*Me*."

"I just... I can't believe you're really here. What are you doing back...?"

She reached forward and cupped a hand around each of his cheeks. "Making a life. And I'm hoping it can be with you."

"I'd like that," he said, rising to his feet and picking her up in a strong embrace. "I'd like that very much." He bent down to kiss her, and she let herself melt into his arms.

There would be no more goodbyes. In fact, this was only the beginning. They still had so much more life to live, and they'd finally be doing it together.

Louise and Brady are getting married! And one of Louise's best friends might just find love at the wedding...

CLICK HERE to get your copy of *In Love with the Pastor*, so that you can keep reading this series today!

∾

And make sure you're on Melissa's list so that you hear about all her new releases, special giveaways, and other sweet bonuses.

You can do that here: MelStorm.com/gift

WHAT'S NEXT?

Rabbi Heidi Gold isn't looking to settle down, but she's thrilled to officiate her best friend's wedding. While dodging her mother's attempts to throw every single Jewish man at the reception into her path, Heidi nearly gets away unattached until she looks across the dance floor and sees heaven personified in a handsome stranger. Add in a forbidden interfaith attraction and a meddling youth group with good intentions, and away we go.

This quick, light-hearted romance from a New York Times bestselling author is sure to put a smile on your face and a song in your heart!

In Love with the Pastor is now available.

CLICK HERE to get your copy so that you can keep reading this series today!

SNEAK PEEK

Josephine Hannah gathered her hair into a ponytail and tucked it into a plain black ski hat. After adding a thick scarf she'd picked up at Target and a pair of sport sunglasses, she was ready to hit the town.

Of course, the hat made her itch and the scarf felt way too warm around her neck, but that was the necessary price of fame. What had life even been like before she had to don a ridiculous disguise just to run out for a cup of coffee?

Josephine could scarcely remember.

Even worse than the costume was the jarring nickname the press had chosen for her—*Jo-Han*. It felt too cutesy, like she'd forever be relegated to romantic comedies and never even get the chance to be considered for a critical, dramatic role.

Romantic comedies were fine as far as movies went. She loved watching them, but the acting took some serious chops, which no one quite realized or appreciated. Especially since her most recent relationship had just gone up in flames for all the world to see.

She'd fallen hard and fast for the leading man in her last production, and while she was more of an up-and-coming Hollywood sensation, he was practically celebrity royalty. *He* never hid from the paparazzi. In fact, he took every opportunity to get both of them noticed.

The press pursued Josephine extra hard because of her good girl image. It seemed as though nothing would give them greater pleasure than seeing her mess up and her reputation take a nosedive. And her ex John loved all the added attention.

"They need to see you constantly. Otherwise they'll forget who you are, Jo-Han," he'd explained with a hammy grin as they walked down the streets of L.A. hand in hand with a trail of mosquitos bobbing after them.

Yes, mosquitos with constantly flashing cameras and invasive, probing questions.

Paparazzi seemed too sophisticated a word for the crowd of gossip rag reporters who accosted her every chance they got. That's why Jo had opted to take it out of the Italian and go with the English "mosquitos." A more perfect metaphor had never been made, least of all by her.

Jo herself was perfect at reciting the words that had been written for her. She could add the exact blend of emotional intensity and strong diction that made casting directors fall all over themselves to land her. But in real life—if there even was still such a thing for Jo—she was terribly, *terribly* shy.

And it made all the attention that much harder.

Her current project had brought her out of Los Angeles, away from New York, and straight to the wilds of Anchorage. Maybe "wilds" wasn't the right way to describe Alaska's biggest city, but compared to her usual haunts, this sweet, snowy town felt like the boonies.

And she loved it already.

"One caramel macchiato please," she told the barista at Starbucks, happily relieved when she wasn't recognized by her now-famous voice. No one recognized her as she waited for her order to come up at the end counter, either.

Could this place actually be heaven?

She took her drink outside and walked through

the streets downtown, stopping occasionally to window shop. As she glanced into the storefront of a little clothing boutique, the worker inside smile and waved.

Oh, no. I've been found out!

Josephine put her head down and rushed for the crosswalk so she could make her escape. She'd only parked a couple of blocks away. If she ran fast, she could make it before the swarm descended.

Before she could even reach the stoplight, however, her heel snagged on the sidewalk and she fell face forward to the ground. Worse than the pain that shot through her ankle was knowing that this little mishap would be all over the nightly news. How embarrassing!

The shopkeeper from the boutique raced her way. "Are you okay?" she cried. "That spill looked super painful."

"I'm fine," she sobbed, searching the ground for her sunglasses, which had skittered off during her fall. "But please leave me alone. I just want to enjoy a normal day about town."

The woman's brows knitted in confusion. "If that's what you want, but can I help you back on your feet first?" She glanced down at Josephine curiously, then offered a hand.

"Don't you want to take my picture?" Jo asked, astonished it hadn't happened already.

"I want to help you. That's all."

Josephine reluctantly took the shopkeeper's hand. Maybe she didn't watch many movies, or read magazines, or...

Pain ripped through her and she fell back to the ground, almost bringing the other woman down with her.

"Oh, gosh!" the shopkeeper cried. "It might be broken. I'm calling an ambulance!"

"Please hurry," Josephine urged. This woman might not recognize her, but it didn't mean that others wouldn't. The longer she sat crumpled on the ground, the more she had a chance to get discovered—and mocked.

Maybe she didn't like Anchorage so much after all.

Dan Rockwell flipped on the siren and directed his ambulance toward the intersection at Minnesota and Northern Lights. Normally this time of year he stayed busy with hunting accidents and your run-of-the-mill medical emergencies. It was kind of unusual to get the first slip and fall of the season weeks before first snow, but hey, any run beat waiting around at the station for something—*anything*—to happen.

As a firefighter-paramedic, Dan lived for the thrill and loved knowing he was not just making a difference in people's lives, but literally saving them every time he signed in for a shift. And, oh, the stories he had to tell from his adventures!

He'd treated gun wounds, rescued cats from trees, and even helped to calm a blaze set at a dog-fighting ring hidden in plain sight within a Mountain View strip mall. Dan never knew what he was going to get each day, and he wouldn't have it any other way.

Pulling up on W. 29th Street now, he had to do a double take. His slip and fall wasn't some little old lady, but rather a gorgeous woman he guessed to be somewhere in her twenties. Even with the thick hat, scarf, and sunglasses hiding her features, he could still make out high cheekbones, a pert nose, full lips, and the graceful body of a ballet dancer.

Which made it all the more strange that she'd somehow managed to slip on pure concrete and now couldn't get up without the aid of an ambulance.

"Thank goodness you're here!" a middle-aged blonde woman shouted as Dan hopped down from his vehicle. "She's been hysterical, and for some reason she's quite afraid. I don't know if someone is maybe chasing her or what, but she keeps looking over her shoulder like she expects something awful to happen."

Dan stole another glance at the woman on the pavement. She didn't look like a victim of domestic violence, but then again, looks could be deceiving. Whatever the reason behind her injuries, he'd be sure to treat her to the best of his ability and offer her a safe place if she needed it.

"You did the right thing by calling us," he said. "We've got it from here."

The caller nodded and backed away to watch from the shelter of an awning.

"Let's go see what we've got." He motioned for his partner, Ted, to follow him, and together the two tall uniformed men marched toward the slight woman crouched on the pavement and clutching at her ankle.

"Good afternoon, Miss," Dan said, always minding his manners. "We're here to help."

"I didn't want a scene," she sobbed. Standing close to her now, Dan saw that a stubborn tear had fallen from beneath her glasses and onto her cheek. "Can we do this somewhere else?"

"Let's get her into the back of the ambulance," Ted said with a nod to Dan.

Dan reached down to offer his hands and help her up, and she accepted with only a brief moment's hesitation. As she rose to her feet, her sunglasses clattered to the ground revealing sharp green eyes, the likes of which Dan had only seen one other time.

"I've got the glasses," Ted said. "You get her inside."

She kept her head angled down, refusing to make eye contact with Dan or anyone else who was watching the scene unfold before them.

"So, how long have you been in Anchorage, Josephine?" he whispered, keeping his face neutral so as not to notify others of the star among them.

Her head jerked up to reveal a face chock full of emotions—everything from embarrassment to fear and maybe even a little gratitude, too.

So this is why the much acclaimed Josephine Hannah was such a great actress—because she truly felt the full gamut of emotions and apparently knew how to call them on cue. He watched as she settled her features into a neutral mask once again, but it was too late.

He'd seen her vulnerability, the real person that lay hidden beneath designer labels, paid endorsements, and scripted performances. He saw Josephine Hannah, and she was far more beautiful than he ever could have imagined.

In Love with the Pastor is now available.

CLICK HERE to get your copy so that you can keep reading this series today!

MORE FROM MELISSA STORM

The Sunday Potluck Club

This group of friends met in the cancer ward of the local hospital. They've been there for each other through the hard times. Now it's time to heal...

Home Sweet Home

The Sunday Potluck Club

Wednesday Walks and Wags

Manic Monday, Inc.

~

The Church Dogs of Charleston

A very special litter of Chihuahua puppies born on Christmas day is adopted by the local church and immediately set to work as tiny therapy dogs.

Lowcountry Life

Lowcountry Love

Lowcountry Legacy

Alaskan Hearts: Sled Dogs

Get ready to fall in love with a special pack of working and retired sled dogs, each of whom change their new owners' lives for the better.

The Loneliest Cottage

The Brightest Light

The Truest Home

The Darkest Hour

Alaskan Hearts: Memory Ranch

This sprawling ranch located just outside Anchorage helps its patients regain their lives, love, and futures.

The Sweetest Memory

The Strongest Love

The Happiest Place

The First Street Church Romances

Sweet and wholesome small town love stories with the community church at their center make for the perfect feel-good reads!

The Reluctant Florist

The Second-Chance Waitress

The Sunday School Teacher

The Summer Bride

The Lonesome Librarian

∼

The Alaska Sunrise Romances

Brothers, sisters, cousins, and friends—are all about to learn that love has a way of finding you when you least expect it.

In Love with the Veterinarian

In Love with the Ski Instructor

In Love with the Slacker

In Love with the Nerd

In Love with the Doctor

In Love with the Football Player

In Love with the Rodeo Rider

In Love with the Pastor

In Love with the Paramedic

Stand-Alone Novels and Novellas

Whether climbing ladders in the corporate world or taking care of things at home, every woman has a story to tell.

Saving Sarah

A Mother's Love

A Colorful Life

Love & War

MEET THE AUTHOR

Melissa Storm loves a good cry. She believes, that whether happy or sad, tears have a way of cleansing the soul. Perhaps that's why her books have been known to make readers grab the nearest box of tissues and clutch it tight while visiting her fictional worlds. Hey, happily ever afters mean that much more when they're hard won, right?

As a *New York Times* and multiple *USA Today* bestselling author, Melissa is always juggling at least half a dozen new story ideas at any given time. She is married to fellow author Falcon Storm, mom to a precocious human princess, and keeper to an entire domestic zoo full of very spoiled cats and canines. Melissa is the owner of Sweet Promise Press, LitRing, Novel Publicity, and Your Author Engine, and also writes under the names of Molly Fitz and Mila Riggs.

Are you ready to ride this emotional roller coaster? Just turn that first page, and hang on tight!

Connect with Melissa

Or sign up for my newsletter and receive an exclusive free story, *Angels in Our Lives*, along with new release alerts, themed giveaways, and uplifting messages from Melissa!

melstorm.com/gift

Or maybe you'd like to chat with other animal-loving readers as well as to learn about new books and give-aways as soon as they happen! Come join Melissa's VIP reader group on Facebook.

melstorm.com/group